THE BEAT

Suspects

"Hey, babe!" Mark called out, optimistically. She caught the side profile of his famous grin. He was looking at the bed, which was empty. His expression changed to puzzlement and he turned towards the bathroom. Then he seemed to sense her behind him. The grin returned.

"Trying to surprise me?" He turned around, full of charm. For a moment, his eyes lit up. Then he saw what she was holding and flinched. Too late. The blow struck him on the side of the head. Mark flopped soundlessly on to the thick-pile carpet where his left leg twitched and his lips let out a gross, gurgling sound. When he was still, she stepped over his limp body and went into the bathroom.

Visit David Belbin's homepage at
http://www.geocities.com/SoHo/Lofts/5155

POINT CRIME

THE BEAT

Suspects

David Belbin

SCHOLASTIC

For Fran

Scholastic Children's Books
Commonwealth House, 1–19 New Oxford Street,
London WC1A 1NU, UK
a division of Scholastic Ltd
London ~ New York ~ Toronto ~ Sydney ~ Auckland
Mexico City ~ New Delhi ~ Hong Kong

First published in the UK by Scholastic Ltd, 1999

Copyright © David Belbin, 1999

ISBN 0 590 11290 2

Typeset by TW Typesetting, Midsomer Norton, Somerset

Printed by Cox & Wyman Ltd, Reading, Berks.

10 9 8 7 6 5 4 3 2 1

PROLOGUE

The door was open, just like he'd said it would be. The hotel had good security. But it couldn't protect Mark Murray from himself.

He deserved what he had coming. How many women had Mark seduced, then thrown aside, or worse? How many would rejoice when they heard that he was dead?

Waiting, wondering about this, she realized that he wasn't worth it. No man was. But what other options were there? A tabloid exposé? Scandals faded within days. If you were rich, or famous, there was no need to feel shame these days. People queued up to forgive you, whether you were the President of the United States or a minor celebrity soap opera star.

Footsteps in the corridor. She tensed up, back

against the wall, as the door opened. Mark stepped inside.

"Hey, babe!" he called out, optimistically. She caught the side profile of his famous grin. Mark was looking at the bed, which was empty. His expression changed to puzzlement and he turned towards the bathroom. Then he seemed to sense her behind him. The grin returned.

"Trying to surprise me?" He turned around, full of charm. For a moment, his eyes lit up. Then he saw what she was holding and flinched. Too late. The blow struck him on the side of the head. Mark flopped soundlessly on to the thick-pile carpet where his left leg twitched and his lips let out a gross, gurgling sound. When he was still, she stepped over his limp body and went into the bathroom.

Taking her time, she used toilet paper to wipe the blood from her face and arms, then flushed the used tissue away. She examined the white tiles carefully to ensure that she had left no traces. That done, she returned to the bedroom. The carpet was thick with blood now: a red so dark that it was almost black. Mark's head was all caved in. There was no need to check his pulse. She dressed, then picked up the murder weapon, which went into a plastic bag she'd brought along specially.

With gloved hands, she locked the door behind her, putting the *do-not-disturb* sign on the handle.

Nobody saw her leave.

1

It was Clare's mum's idea to go to the theatre. The last time Clare had been to the Theatre Royal was a school trip to see *Macbeth* with Pete Postlethwaite in the title role. But Mum was curious to see Mark Murray making his big stage début.

Clare wasn't bothered about Mark. She didn't watch the soap opera which he used to star in. The irregular hours she worked put the kibosh on seeing any regular TV shows. Nor did she know Murray well, though she'd seen him around often enough when they were growing up. His mum was friendly with her mum. A year older than her, he'd always been fond of himself, with his blue eyes and boy band looks. Too fond, as far as Clare was concerned.

Clare hadn't been out much lately. An ankle

injury – nearly a month ago now – had kept her off work, and she was still walking with a stick. Her best friend, Ruth, had just lost her father and was taking time off from the force to be with her mum. Clare's boyfriend – the man she'd meant to marry – had been killed in early October. It was now mid-November and Clare still woke up some mornings expecting to find him in bed next to her. So, a play, why not? She'd do anything to take her mind off murder.

Clare dressed carefully, choosing a loose silk blouse which concealed the weight she'd put on while she'd been off work (Mum's cooking combined with lack of exercise: fatal). Tonight, Mum looked good, better than Clare. You'd never guess that she was the wrong side of forty. At least, not unless someone told you that Clare, twenty-one, was her daughter. Mum and Dad had been separated for two months now. It briefly occurred to Clare that other men might take an interest in Maria Coppola. But no. Mum wasn't ready, any more than Clare was.

They got to the Theatre Royal with several minutes to spare. Mum went to order an interval drink. Sam, Clare's landlady, joined her. With her was Steve, an amateur actor and reformed thief.

"When are you moving back in?" Sam asked. Clare had been staying with her mum since the accident.

"Soon, I guess. Maybe… Hey, what's *he* doing here?"

He was Neil Foster, a CID officer and an ex of Clare's. Neil had never been to the theatre in his life. Clare would be surprised if he knew what one was. Yet there he was, accompanied by Chris Dylan, who was his immediate superior. Both men wore the badly cut suits which indicated that they were on duty.

"Why don't you ask him?" Sam said. "I'm getting a programme." Clare stood up straighter to flatten her stomach, then waved to Neil. Seeing her, he nodded, but made no attempt to join her.

"I don't believe it!" Sam said. "Look at this." A slip had been inserted in the programme. It read *In tonight's performance the role of Martin Plummer will be taken by Jeremy Eaton.*

"That's Mark's part! He's not in it." Clare shrugged. She wasn't that bothered. But Mum would be.

"Bad news," she called, as Mum returned from the bar. "Mark's ill." Mum swore. "Kathy'll be so disappointed."

That was Mark's mum. They were meant to be sitting with her. Only, when they took their seats in the front stalls, Kathy Murray was nowhere to be seen.

Mark Murray's understudy was pretty good, actually. Better than Murray might have been in the role, Steve guessed. He had it in for people who succeeded effortlessly in the acting world. Mark Murray had gone from nowhere to soap opera stardom in the space of six months. A small part had turned into a big one. Then, a year later, Murray had been confident enough to quit the soap. He wanted to do theatre, he said, maybe movies. And he would probably make it. Whereas Steve had been at it for a year now and hadn't even found himself an agent. Steve got by on the dole and with subs from his parents, plus free drinks and meals from his girlfriend, Sam. She'd even taken him on holiday once.

At least Steve had managed to keep away from thieving for a while. His past remained a problem. If employers asked, he couldn't produce a certificate to show that he was conviction free. He wasn't. However, in acting, a criminal past didn't matter. It even looked good in interviews. But, first, you had to get the parts. Steve had only just managed to attain his Equity card. That was the result of months doing small scale, self-financed productions in pubs up and down the county. Mark Murray was Steve's age. But he was famous. So famous that he could afford to blow out a performance, probably because he had a hangover. Steve was jealous as hell.

On stage, Martin – the character who Mark should have been playing – was threatening to blackmail a married man who he'd been having an affair with. Steve could do that. He could play gay, even though he was no more homosexual than Murray. You got to see Martin naked, from behind. Steve could do that, too. He wouldn't be embarrassed. Well, maybe a bit, seeing as he was naked with Anna Derbyshire, an actress who, in Steve's book, personified the word "tasty".

The play was lively but predictable. There were meaty parts for the male and female leads, but the story was a run of the mill one about drugs and sex, full of empty sneers about government hypocrisy. Geoff Darlington did a tired job as a corrupt Government minister in a *ménage à trois* with Anna Derbyshire and Jeremy Eaton. The set resembled nothing more than a fifties' kitchen-sink drama. Steve had read enough work by young playwrights to know where this one was heading, towards a fashionably bleak conclusion. Still, he wished he was in it.

"I'm rather glad it isn't Mark," Mum whispered in Clare's ear. "I don't think I'd be able to face Kathy after seeing him like that."

"We are awfully close to the stage," Clare acknowledged, as they got up at the interval. She glanced into the nearest box. There, pouring champagne, was one of the city's top lawyers, a solicitor called Ian Jagger. Clare gasped. Jagger's companion was one of his employees, Charlene

Harris, a dazzling-looking black woman, half his age. The way she leant towards him as he poured left no doubt in Clare's mind: their relationship was more than a professional one. Did Ben know that they were seeing each other? Her colleague, Ben Shipman, had gone out with Charlene for nearly five years. And he hated Ian Jagger.

Sitting further back in the next box was her work colleague and fellow lodger, Gary Monk. He was filling the wine glass of his boyfriend, Umberto Capricio. Clare leant into the box.

"Fancy seeing you here."

"Clare!" Umberto gave her a kiss, then retreated to the rear of the box. He and Gary had to be discreet. Famous footballers weren't meant to be gay. Nor, if they wanted respect, were police officers. But Clare had helped bring the two men together and both were very fond of her. She introduced her mother.

"Would you like to join us?" Umberto offered. "There's plenty of room in here."

"We've got a very good view as it is," Mum said. "I wish I knew what had happened to Mark though. I was so looking forward to—"

"But the understudy is so much better looking!" Umberto interrupted, and they all laughed. Actually, Clare did quite fancy the understudy, a tall thin youth with closely cropped hair.

"We'd better get to our drinks," she said. "See you after, maybe."

"When are you coming back to work?" Gary called after her.

"I'm seeing the doctor in the morning."

As they left the stalls, Clare observed that Neil and Dylan were still around, pointing and note-taking. What on earth were they doing here?

"Don't tell me," she teased the sergeant five minutes later. "You're investigating a scam where people sneak into the theatre without paying."

"That's impossible tonight," Dylan said. "The play's sold out."

"So were you looking to arrest one of the audience? What's going on?"

"Tell you later," Dylan said. "Sorry, duck, but it's a bit sensitive." Clare frowned. Not long ago, she'd been attached to CID, in on everything. Now she was an ordinary plod again. Less than a plod, she thought, as she leant on her stick and sipped vodka and tonic. She was on the sick and out of mind.

"What do you think of it so far?" Steve asked.

"Rubbish," Clare replied, because the question and answer was one of her dad's catchphrases. Steve didn't get the joke.

"I don't think it's that bad," he said. "Interesting approach to sexuality." And then he was off, his conversation reminding her that he'd finished a University degree and she hadn't. Once, Steve had been interested in her and she'd been tempted, until she found that he was a small-time burglar. Luckily for Steve, Sam wasn't so choosy.

Mum rejoined them. "I just rang Kathy," she said. "She sounded in a state. 'It's bad,' she said. 'I'm not allowed to tell anybody yet. Sorry. But it's bad.' What on earth do you think she was talking about?"

"Dunno," Clare said, as they went in to watch the second half of the play. She didn't want Mum to worry. It sounded like Mark was seriously ill. Or in trouble. That *not allowed* was particularly ominous. She found it hard to concentrate on the second half.

2

"What's *she* doing here?" Detective Inspector Greasby asked, pointing at Clare Coppola in the Theatre Royal bar.

"Friend of the family," Neil explained.

"Friend, eh," Greasby muttered to himself. "Might be useful." Neil watched as the DI tapped Clare on the shoulder. A minute later, he was being introduced to Clare's mother. Neil groaned. He could see it coming. The DI had a soft spot for Clare. Soon, she would be helping out with the investigation. Fine for Clare. But Neil didn't like to work closely with her. He was over her, had a six-month-old relationship with Melanie, a university student. But Clare was the first big love of Neil's life, a love he could do without being reminded of every single working day.

Greasby rejoined him.

"We're in luck. There's another probationer here tonight – what was it, cheap tickets or something? – Gary Monk. We can use him and Clare to interview some of the minor characters."

"Where are we going to take them? Central station?"

"With all the drunks and domestics? Nah. We'll use the hotel. But discreetly. I don't want the news of this to get out yet. We could do with some quiet time to pull the threads together before all hell breaks loose."

The cast were starting to filter into the bar for a drink.

"Is that normal?" Neil asked the theatre manager. "The actors mingling with the audience after a show?"

"In the provinces and smaller places, sure. Even quite big names … 'scuse me." Two teenage girls had appeared in the doorway at the far end of the bar, glammed up, looking around expectantly. The manager went over to them.

"That was easier than normal," he said, returning to the officers. "Told them Mark Murray was off sick and they left."

"Did Murray come in here after the play?" Neil asked.

"First night, I think he met a friend here. But there was a bit of a scrum around him and the pair of them left, went somewhere quieter. Last night, no."

"The friend's name?"

"No idea. He was about Murray's age. Someone local, I suppose."

"Anyone else here tonight who you saw talking to Murray?"

"Apart from the cast, no."

"Excuse me." A tousled-haired northerner interrupted them. "Hi, George."

"Dan." The manager introduced the guy as a reporter from the *Evening Post*. How had they got on to this so quickly? "What can I do for you?"

"I need to know why Mark Murray was off tonight. We had a couple of phone calls, disappointed punters, you know the sort of thing."

"He was indisposed."

"Come on, George, it's a story. If he's got a cold, people want to know. Question is, will he be back tomorrow?"

"It's too early to say."

The reporter looked Neil up and down. "You're CID, aren't you?"

"Do we give off some special kind of smell?" Neil asked.

"Is there a story here, or what?"

Neil lowered his voice. "There's been a spate of bag thefts in the Ladies, if you must know. I've got an officer working undercover. But we don't need publicity or you might scare the thief away."

"Fair enough. Here, have my card. Call me if you catch her. I'll give you a good write-up, detective ... what's your name?" Neil told him, then looked at the name on the card, Dan Rossiter.

"Thanks," he said to the manager when the reporter was gone. "I thought he was on to the murder."

"We rely on good relations with the press," the manager pointed out. "Someone's bound to give them the story tomorrow. You'd probably get better co-operation if it were you."

"Point taken," Neil said. "I'll mention it to my superiors. Now, we need to round up the cast." But before he could get to them, he saw Clare.

"Aren't you going to tell me what's going on?" she asked.

"All right," Neil told her. "Over here."

They found a quiet, circular sitting area beyond the box office. Neil whispered.

"Mark Murray's dead."

"Working?" Mum asked, incredulous. "But you're on the sick. You don't even see the doctor 'til tomorrow."

"And we know what he'll say," Clare told her. "Same as last week. 'You're ready to go back, but confined to desk duties until Christmas. Or, if you're still feeling depressed, I'll give you a certificate for another week.' I *am* feeling depressed. But desk duties will make me feel worse. Whereas John Greasby's offering me a chance to be in on an investigation."

"What investigation?" Mum asked. "I don't understand. Is it connected with Mark, him being missing tonight?"

Clare lowered her voice. "Yes, Mum, I'm afraid it is. But I can't tell you until tomorrow. And I'm going to be out late. Give Sam and Steve a lift home, why don't you?" She thought of asking Mum to take her stick with her. Clare could get by without it. But that would be silly, pure vanity. What if she stumbled or slipped? She could put herself back weeks.

When Mum had gone Clare went over in her head what Neil had told her about Mark's death. The actor had been seen coming into his hotel just before five. The stage manager had called his room at the hotel at twenty past and then twenty-five past seven, wanting to know why Mark hadn't arrived at the theatre. When there was no reply the second time, she'd spoken to the hotel manager, who'd used a pass key to let himself into the room at seven thirty precisely. There, he found that somebody had given the actor a lethal blow to the head with a heavy object.

Clare joined Gary, who told her that the two CID men had gone to the cast's hotel.

"We're to stay on here," he continued. "Talk to

the front of house staff, see if they noticed anything suspicious. Then we head to the hotel, join Neil and Chris."

"Do the cast know yet?" Clare asked.

"No. Greasby thinks it better if we wait until they're back at the hotel. The story's less likely to leak out."

"Why the big secrecy?" Clare wanted to know.

"It'll be a circus, won't it?" Gary suggested. "Media everywhere. People selling their story to the press before they talk to us, corrupted evidence, the lot."

Was Mark Murray that big a star? Clare wondered. To her, he was an overgrown schoolboy, too arrogant for his own good. He had touched her up once, when she was thirteen. She'd done what Mum had told her to do in such a situation and kneed him in the groin. He'd yelped. After the pain subsided, he'd given her a funny look, as though she ought to have been flattered that he thought her worth groping.

After that, whenever she'd seen Mark, he'd been hidden behind that smug mask of his, the girl on his arm always thinner and better looking than Clare. The irony was that if he'd asked her out instead of feeling her up, Clare might have said yes. Later, when she saw what a user he was, Clare was glad that she'd acted as she did, not made a fool of herself, like every girl he dated. When he did see her, at family events, Mark skirted Clare with wary respect. He used women, like half the men she knew. That was a bad thing, sure. But was it, Clare wondered, what got him killed?

Gary assumed that the Royal Court toured with a huge retinue of people. He was wrong, as Jane Waverly, the stage manager, explained.

"It's just me and the actors. The theatres we go to deal mainly with touring productions, so they have a full time, permanent staff."

"What about the director?"

"His job's done. Oh, he may look in from time to time, give notes to make sure that the whole thing's not gone slack. Mainly, though, that's down to me."

"So there are only five of you?"

"Seven. There are understudies for the two main parts. Most small scale plays don't bother with understudies these days, but they're only paid the Equity minimum. Paying an understudy is a lot cheaper than cancelling a performance."

"Are the stars of this play more prone to missing performances than most?" Jane smiled diplomatically. "Well, Mark and Anna are both from TV, though Anna's done a lot of stage work. Mark hasn't, so that's an immediate risk, yes. But he hasn't missed a performance until today. Is Mark what this is about?"

"Yes."

"What's happened?"

"I'm not at liberty to say. How do you get on with him?" Jane thought for a moment. Deciding whether to be diplomatic, Gary guessed.

"Mark's a pro. As an actor, he's given me no problems at all."

"What about as a bloke?"

"His reputation goes before him. One of those thinks-he's-God's-gift types. Doesn't like taking no for an answer."

"Did he try it on with you?" Gary asked, surprised. Waverly was thirtyish. Nice figure, but nothing special to look at. Too old for Murray, surely? But Jane looked bashful and he realized that he was wrong.

"In the first week he made a pass, yes. In the interval, would you believe? Maybe he thought that all that naked flesh would turn me on. Or maybe it turned him on."

"What did he say?"

"'How about a quickie?' Something like that."

"And when you turned him down?"

"What makes you think I turned him down?" she asked, a twinkle in her eye.

Gary blushed. "Sorry, I … from what you said, I assumed…"

Jane laughed. "No need to be embarrassed. You're right. I told him I was married. He said, 'So what?' Then I walked away. End of story."

"You weren't offended?"

She shrugged. "I think I was meant to be flattered. Offended? No. Irritated, yes. We were in the middle of a play. He was like a big kid, asking for a lollipop when he knew it was wrong to eat between meals."

"Did you at any time see anyone hanging around Mark, showing an unusual degree of interest?"

"There were teenage girls by the stage doors all day the last three days. Apart from that, no."

"Thanks," Gary said. "You've been very helpful. If you think of anything else…"

"Aren't you going to tell me what he's done?"

"You'll find out soon enough," Gary assured her.

He joined Clare in the otherwise empty Theatre Royal bar. It was nearly midnight. Only a security man remained on duty.

"Get anything good?" she asked.

"Not really. You?"

"Nope. Is there an incident room set up yet?"

"No, we're to go over to their hotel, report back. I can pass on your bits and pieces if you're feeling too knackered."

"You're kidding," Clare said. "On the sick, I doze so much during the day that I have trouble getting off at night. And I knew Mark. I want in on this."

"Better make tracks then." They called the security man and he let them out. At the door, Gary paused. "Has someone interviewed you?" he asked the man, who looked more like a bouncer than a caretaker.

" 'Bout what?"

"Mark Murray."

"What's he done?"

"Have you had any contact with him?" Gary asked, ignoring the question as Clare waited impatiently in the cold November air.

"I have, as it happens. Yesterday, there was a gang of girls waiting for him after the show. And he was going off to meet someone. So I showed him the side way out. Mind you, there was still a girl hanging round out there."

"Can you describe her?"

"Long blonde hair. A looker. Seventeen, maybe. Couldn't say more."

"Do you remember anything else Mark said or did?"

"Asked the way to some restaurant. Stoke … somethin'. I'd never heard of it."

"Stokely's?" Clare suggested.

"That's it. I didn't know where it was but the girl, she said she'd show him the way. So they went off together, up the hill."

"Thanks," Gary said. "You've been very helpful."

"What do you reckon?" Gary asked Clare. "Go to this restaurant?"

"It's not far," Clare said. "A small place, beyond Trent university."

"A student haunt?"

"No. Too expensive. Paul took me once. French food."

"Think there'll still be somebody there?"

"If you hurry, yes. If you wait for me to trudge along, no. I'll meet you at the hotel."

"All right. Tell the boss where I am." He walked up South Sherwood Street, wondering who Mark Murray had met for dinner.

3

Neil's first interview was with the male under-study, Jeremy Eaton. This wasn't because he was the biggest suspect, but because he was the only one downstairs when the three officers arrived at the hotel.

"We could go to your room," Neil told him. "Get some privacy."

"My room's smaller than a police cell. Can't we talk down here?"

"I guess."

They found a quiet corner of the hotel bar. Eaton was wiry, with sunken eyes and short cropped hair. Neil recalled seeing him playing a psychotic skin-head on TV.

"What's happened to Mark?" Jeremy asked. "This is about Mark, isn't it?"

"I'm afraid I can't give you any details yet," Neil said. "Can I ask a few questions? It shouldn't take long."

Jeremy Eaton turned out to be twenty, with two years' professional acting experience, mostly in non-speaking parts or as an understudy. He'd done a little TV. He had a chip on his shoulder, Neil gathered, which was hardly surprising. Many actors came from privileged backgrounds which helped them to support themselves during the inevitable long periods of unemployment. Jeremy had been brought up in a children's home since the age of eight, had left school at sixteen, had even been briefly homeless before landing a job as an extra on a TV ad. Slowly – the way he told it – he had, through persistence more than anything else, achieved a tenuous hold on the first rungs of the acting ladder.

"Can you tell me where you were between four and seven today?" Neil asked, once this background had been established.

"Sleeping. Here. I always have a sleep before a performance. Helps to keep me calm, focused."

"But you're an understudy. You weren't performing."

"You never know though, do you? Anyway, I still have a job to do, carrying stuff on and off stage. It's in the public eye."

"Did anyone see you here during that time?"

"Why would they?"

"What w— is your relationship with Mark Murray like?"

"What relationship? He's not interested in the likes of me. Look, this is the third week of the tour. All the guy really seems interested in after a show is pulling. Some actors, they go on the road, they're like freed animals, know what I mean?"

"Will it be good for your career, doing his part?"

"For one night? Hardly. If he was gone for the rest of the run and I could get a few producers, directors, agents to see me, then, sure ... but that's not going to happen, is it? What's he done, anyway?"

"Sorry," Neil said. "I can't tell you that."

The restaurant was closed, but the owners lived above the place in a small but elegant flat. Penelope, who was front of house, remembered Mark Murray. Who wouldn't?

"I got him to pose for a photo with Jake." Jake was her husband, the chef. Real name, Penelope confided, Jacques: a genuine French chef.

"You didn't get a picture of his companion?"

"No. Sorry."

"What was she like?"

"The one he came with or the one he met?"

"How do you mean? 'The one he came with'?"

"It was quite embarrassing, actually," Penelope

said. "The woman he was meeting had booked the table, so we didn't know who to expect. But she got here first, told us who he was and that they'd like a quiet table. I gave them the one in the corner. That's where we normally put couples who act like they're doing something they shouldn't be. Anyway, Mark Murray arrives with a young bird in tow – sixteen or seventeen, I'd say – takes a quick look through the window to see if his date is there, but doesn't notice her. So he steps round the corner and necks the seventeen year old for a good two minutes before coming in. His date saw him with her, though, and must have had a pretty good idea what he was doing."

"Did they argue?"

"No. She acted like it hadn't happened. And so did I, of course. You have to pretend to be blind and deaf all the time in this game. When he came in he was all smiles and hugs. But she looked a little frosty all evening, I must say."

"What time did they leave?"

"Early, considering it was a post-theatre meal. Eleven-thirty, something like that. We called a taxi for them. She got in it, drove off. He walked away in the opposite direction. That's everything. Now, are you going to tell me what this is about?"

"Can't, I'm sorry. You say the woman booked the meal?"

"Yes."

"Would you have her name recorded somewhere?"

"In the book downstairs, yes."

"Do you take a phone number when people make a booking?"

"I do. But I should warn you, it won't be any use to you."

"Why not?" Gary asked.

"Because the name she gave was Smith and the phone number is bound to be fake, too."

"I don't under—"

"She was married. She hadn't even bothered to take off her ring."

Neil recognized the actress. According to the programme which Clare had given him, Anna Derbyshire had done two years with the Royal Shakespeare Company, three British feature films, and a "leading role" in an as yet unseen TV series about women in the First World War. But Neil knew her from *The Zoo Crew*, a children's TV show which Anna starred in when Neil was twelve or thirteen. Anna would have been about fifteen then. She was slight, with huge eyes and thin, delicate, fair hair. Then, he'd had a bit of a pre-pubescent crush on her. Now, she was in her mid to late twenties. The fair hair was darker, and tied back, but she was still drop-dead gorgeous.

"What's happened to Mark?" she asked, with a slight Geordie accent.

"It's not good," Neil told her.

"What does that mean?"

"I'm not at liberty to say at this moment. Were you and he … friends?" Anna shrugged. "Mates, I suppose. You have to be when you work as closely together as we do. Have you seen the play?"

"No," Neil admitted.

"Ask anyone who has. They'll tell you what I mean."

"I'm asking you," Neil insisted.

She raised her eyebrows in a look of studied shamelessness. "We get naked together," she told him. "Just a quick glimpse at the end of the first act, but it gets us a lot of repeat business from the dirty raincoat brigade."

Neil blushed. "I didn't realize that it was so raunchy," he said. "Do you mind me asking, were you and he…?"

She picked up his slip instantly. "*Were*. Do you mean that he's…?"

"I'm not at liberty to—"

"—*say*, I'm an actor, I know the lines. Has someone done for him?" *Done for*. People didn't say that much any more, Neil thought, except in plays.

"Were you and Mark…" Anna Derbyshire frowned that famous frown which Neil used to find so impressive when she was starring in *The Zoo Crew*. Then she took a deep breath.

"Before you go any further, I'd better tell you that

27

I'm gay. Mark knew that, though it didn't stop him trying once."

"I can't imagine he got knocked back often," Neil commented.

"Why?" Anna challenged him. "You think that just because a man's good-looking and on the telly, any woman'll drop her knickers for him? Not true. I've watched Mark on the pull. He probably gets turned down two times out of three. But that only spurs him on. He's like a gambler chasing a winning bet. And he prefers a challenge. Less interested in the girls who hung around the stage door, than in the married ones, the ones with steady boyfriends. Anyone half attractive who wasn't interested or impressed by him, he'd have a go. In a nice way – he never offended anyone, far as I could see. He was quite a piece of work, I'll tell you." She paused. "I said *was*, didn't I?"

"Yes," Neil said. "You did. Do you mind me asking, where you were between four and seven this evening?"

"Oh God," she said, huge eyes growing even bigger. "Someone really has done for him, haven't they?"

Neil Foster had bagged the sexy female lead and the male understudy, so Chris Dylan was left with the female understudy and the leading man. The actor, Geoff Darlington, had little to tell. He didn't know

Mark Murray well, he said. "I got the impression that he didn't have many male friends: far too interested in skirt. You know what they say: you can have a good work life, a passionate love life and a happy social life, but you can't have all three at once. Mark had the first two."

Darlington had a solid looking alibi for the time when Mark Murray died. He was shopping with his wife and two preschool kids, who'd joined him for a day in Nottingham. The kids had a good time looking round the Castle, the caves and the Robin Hood Experience, before returning to London on the 19.03 train. Darlington waved his family off then walked to the Theatre Royal, getting there comfortably in time to dress for the eight o'clock performance.

The understudy's room was less than half the size of Darlington's. Lynda Crabbe was about Chris's age (thirty-two), short haired and pretty. Slightly on the dumpy side for some tastes, perhaps, but Dylan wouldn't kick her out of bed in the morning.

"It's not much of a job," she told him. "But I'm lucky to have the work. Most small touring productions like this don't bother with understudies: too expensive."

"Have you ever had to come on?"

She smiled ruefully. "Not once so far. You spend half your time hoping that somebody you're friendly with catches a cold. Jeremy got lucky tonight. But why did Mark miss the performance? Has he been arrested for something?"

"I'm afraid I'm not allowed to say at the moment. What was … is your relationship with Mark like?" he asked, making a note.

"We're … very friendly." *Oh, oh, here we go*, he thought. He waited for Lynda to continue. She blushed, sensing that she'd already given away the nature of their relationship.

"It was just a one-off," she said. "He's not the sort of bloke who makes commitments to women."

"So I've heard," Chris muttered. He wasn't that sort himself, but most women got upset when you gave them the news; accusing you of being a user or something worse, so he'd learnt to back away with an array of abstract apologies.

"So," he said, "you and Mark had a one-night stand?"

"A brief dalliance," she said, with a relaxed smile.

"Did you use your room or his?" Dylan asked.

"His. As you can see, I don't always get my own shower, never mind a suite."

"And, do you mind me asking, was Mark seeing anyone else on the tour?" Lynda half-smiled. Dylan smiled back, a hint of a flirtation between them. Both knew exactly what the score was. Dylan was in with a chance here. Though the news of Mark

Murray's death wasn't likely to put Lynda in the mood.

"Not as far as I know," she said. "But Mark could be very discreet."

"Thanks," Dylan said, noting her precise words and valuing them. Lynda Crabbe was the sort of woman who sniffed out what was going on.

"Did he see anyone from outside the tour?"

"I really don't know."

"One last question. Could you tell me where you were between four and seven this evening?"

"I went to a movie at the Odeon. What was it called? I think I still have the ticket…" Conveniently, she produced it. "When I got back to the hotel, you lot were already here. If that was your last question, are you going to tell me what Mark's done?"

"I'm sorry," Dylan told her. "I'm not at liberty to."

Neil, Dylan and Greasby were still conducting interviews when Clare got to the hotel. She waited in the lobby, remembering Mark Murray, wondering whether a murder investigation was the best reintroduction to the world of police work.

The three officers arrived in the lobby together.

"There you are," Greasby said. "Why didn't you come up to the incident room?" Of course, the hotel had provided CID with a room to work from. Clare hadn't thought of asking at reception. Before Clare could reply, Gary arrived. He told a story of two women at the restaurant on Tuesday night: one inside, one outside.

"Sounds more interesting than anything we've got," Chris Dylan said. Clare gave them the meagre information they'd picked up at the theatre. Greasby didn't seem impressed.

"Ten to one on this being about sex," he said. "Trouble is, this bloke has more women in a week than Chris here manages in a year." The other three men laughed. Dylan's reputation as a philanderer seemed to be a standing joke in CID. He'd even had a one-night stand with Clare's best friend, Ruth.

"Have the cast all got decent alibis, Sir?" Clare asked, trying to turn the subject back to the murder. Greasby grunted. He was hardly going to tell an off duty plonk if he had a handle on a murderer.

"We've got as far as we're going to get tonight," he said. "We'll have to issue a press statement in the morning. I'd like to see the mother again before the media blitz starts. You're a friend of the family, Clare?"

"My mum's close to his, yes."

"Then I'd like you with me. Meet me at a quarter to ten, right?"

"Sir."

She would have to cancel her doctor's appointment, but it didn't matter. Clare no longer needed a new sick note. The decision had been made for her. She was back.

4

Nobody at school believed Jo.

"You met him? In your dreams. If you saw him, why did Kate and Gemma miss him, huh?"

"I waited at a different exit."

"And how did you know to do that?"

She hadn't known, only guessed that, with twenty or more girls outside, Mark Murray would avoid the stage door. If he had come out and started signing autographs there, rather than doing a runner, she would have heard the commotion and run over in time. As it was, he'd left by another exit, one used for deliveries. Jo had seen some pizzas being delivered there when she was on her vigil the day before.

The stupid thing was, she hadn't got his autograph. The walk to the restaurant had taken the best part of ten minutes, during which they'd been chatting constantly. Jo had replayed that conversation a thousand times already. She'd told Mark how she'd watched him three times a week for the full two years he'd been on the telly, then stopped watching the soap in protest when he left. As soon as she'd heard he was leaving, Jo told him, she'd videoed every remaining episode that he was in, so that she'd have something to watch when he was gone. Mark had laughed.

"Most of them weren't worth watching once, never mind twice," he said. Then he'd asked her what she'd thought of the play and she'd blushed because, in it, he'd been naked. You didn't get to see that much, actually. It was just like in films – the actress gave a full-frontal while you had to settle for the bloke's backside. But it still embarrassed her.

"It was very … explicit," she'd said, proud of remembering the word. And Mark laughed. "You can say that again. You know, my mum's coming to see me tomorrow. I don't know how I'll face her afterwards. I'm thinking of asking for a body double."

"What's one of those?" she'd asked.

"Joanna, have you got your homework?"

"Yes, Mrs Hunt, sorry." Jo got her project out.

She'd been lost in cloud–cuckoo–land since Tuesday night, unable to think straight. She didn't blame her mates for thinking she was making it up, because the whole meeting had felt like a daydream. She'd been chatting to Mark so unselfconsciously. He'd put her at her ease in a way which the handful of boys she'd been out with never could. He'd told her about the woman he was meeting and other family stuff. She'd told him how the boys who asked her out were always yobs. The lads she liked were far too shy to even start a conversation with her. He'd given her some advice on how to get them more relaxed.

And then, oh then, far, far too quickly, they were at the restaurant, and he was thanking her, offering his hand, like a grown-up. That was when she should have shaken it and asked for an autograph. But her love for him had made her brave.

"Giverchisspl," she'd said, the words coming out wrong.

"Pardon," he said, giving her *that* smile, the one she'd freeze-framed so many times.

"Give us a kiss, please," she'd repeated, not garbling the words this time. As she prayed for a peck on the cheek, Mark glanced down the street.

"What," he said, "with the world watching?" She thought he was turning her down, but he took her hand and guided her round the corner, almost beyond the restaurant's bay window. And then, and then…

* * *

Noel Street Baths were slimy green, slippery and in dire need of a face-lift, but the pool was big and the water was clean. That was all that mattered to Clare. The doctor had told her that swimming was the safest form of exercise to repair her damaged ankle. She still worried that someone would knock against it and swam cautiously. This early morning session was women only, though, so relatively safe.

Swimsuit on, she examined herself critically in the mirror before getting in. She was a bit podgy, but nothing a few weeks exercise and a strict diet wouldn't cure. She needed to sort herself out by Christmas, though, or she'd never lose the extra two inches which had appeared around her waist.

Clare did twenty lengths without too much difficulty. After getting dressed, she walked down to Sam's (hard, at the moment, to call it *home*), checked her mail and called a taxi to take her to the Murray house in Wollaton.

There was nothing exciting in the post. Clare went up to her bedroom, where she filed away a bank statement and a demand for part of her student loan which she still hadn't paid off (she'd only done four terms at uni, but was still in debt for it). By the bed was a photo of Paul Grace, taken before she'd met him. Paul, grinning, in an open-necked polo shirt, looked very young and full of optimism. He looked like he was going to take over the world. Instead, he'd taken a bullet to the heart.

Before Clare could get emotional, a taxi sounded its horn outside. She set off to meet the mother whose loss was more recent than hers, and equally violent.

Who had killed Mark Murray? Clare didn't know. Sex was likely to be at the root of it, she guessed. Or not sex as such, but passion, love, call it what you will … she wondered whether Mark had ever been in love with anyone but himself.

Mark had been hit with something heavy and hard, which had not been left at the scene of the crime. The assailant could have been a woman or a man. A jealous husband or a spurned lover – that was the assumption which CID were working on. Major Crimes were looking into the possible burglary angle. There was no sign of forced entry to the room, but that didn't rule out a sneak-thief interrupted in the act.

Clare reminded herself of what Paul used to say: it was important not to jump to conclusions. The autopsy wasn't in yet. There were all sorts of non-sexual motives for murder. If DI Greasby forgot to mention it, Clare must make it clear to Mark's mum that the police had an open mind as to why her son had died.

* * *

Kathy Murray didn't, though.

"All that screwing around! I told him he'd come a cropper, but he never listens. Just like his father, Mark is. Can't resist anything that catches his eye. And if the girl plays hard to get, he likes it all the more. That's why he went into acting, you know, Clare. Nothing to do with art, everything to do with skirt."

In the front room of a semi in genteel Wollaton, Clare nodded and smiled encouragement. Kathy Murray was a little older than Clare's mum. She kept herself smartly turned out, and had not been short of gentlemen callers since her divorce, when Mark was still at Infant School. Today though, her perm was shot to pieces; her clothes hung loosely around her and there were bags beneath her eyes. Kathy was keeping going on coffee, adrenaline and frequent nips of whisky. She had known for fifteen hours that her only son was dead, but had yet to take in the news fully.

"Mark's father," Greasby said, gently. "What happened to him?"

"I threw Ted out when Mark was five. Caught him at it with the babysitter, that was the final straw. She was only fifteen."

"Did he stay in contact?"

"For a couple of years. Then the money stopped coming and so did he."

"No word at all?"

"Not for a good few years now. Story was, he'd married again, divorced again, taken to drink. Last I heard, he'd emigrated to Australia. Good riddance."

"His job?"

"Worked in the building trade when we were together."

"Did he get in touch with Mark when he got on TV?" Clare asked.

"If he did, Mark didn't tell me. I doubt that he knows about it."

"Did Mark make a will?" The DI asked.

"Not as far as I know."

Greasby got the name of the family solicitor so that they could check this out.

"We're going to have to put out a statement to the press," DI Greasby told her. "Are you up to giving a press conference?"

"No. No way," Kathy Murray insisted, becoming tearful again. "I'm in a state. I'm not going on telly."

"You're likely to be under siege from the tabloids, I'm afraid," Greasby told her. "Is there a friend or relative you could stay with until things calm down?"

"There are one or two neighbours…"

"Neighbours aren't a good idea," Greasby said. "Too close by. Word's bound to get out."

"You could stay at ours," Clare told her. "Mum'd

be glad to have you. It's a quiet street. You wouldn't be noticed."

"Oh, thank you, Clare," Kathy said. "If you're sure Maria wouldn't mind…"

"I'll ring her at work," Clare said. "I'm sure it'll be OK."

"Do it now," Greasby told Clare, as Kathy blew her nose. "I want Mrs M out of the way before we tell the press. I plan to go through the *Evening Post* first, then the local telly. If we have them on our side, helping us dig for leads, we might get somewhere before the big boys turn up waving their cheque-books."

"Sounds wise to me," Clare said, then went to use the phone in the hall. Mum had a job in a Travel Agent's. Clare got through to her and asked if she could get off work.

"Why? What's wrong?"

"You musn't tell anybody yet, Mum, but something awful's happened to Mark. Kathy needs a place to stay, somewhere secret, away from the media. Is it all right if she comes to us?"

"Yes, yes, of course it is. Poor … oh, Clare. I'm going to go now. I'll meet you at home, make up the spare room."

"She can have mine," Clare said. "Time I moved out anyway. Got to go."

There, that was another decision made. Back to Sam's. Sad as she was for Kathy, the last thing Clare wanted was to be around a grieving mother all day. Her own loss was too recent for her to selflessly help someone else. Mum had lost a son. She would know what to say to Kathy. It was time for Clare to get on with her life.

Clare returned to the living room and told Kathy Murray to pack enough clothes for a week. Next, Greasby phoned Dan Rossiter at the *Evening Post* and gave him the biggest scoop of his career, just in time for the *City Final* edition. Then, while Kathy was upstairs packing, Clare and the DI discussed the case. Away from other officers, Greasby was more open than the night before.

"No leads?" Clare asked.

"Nothing substantial. We're trying to track down the woman he had dinner with the other night and the girl who he was seen kissing beforehand. Bit difficult to put that in the papers without a scandal though … the woman was married."

"Maybe just a friend."

"That's not how the press will present it." Greasby thought aloud. "As for the girl – she could be anyone. Do we advertise for her, too? Suppose she was the one?"

"He'd hardly have snogged her outside the restaurant if she was likely to be jealous of the woman he was meeting inside," Clare pointed out.

"True. But I think we'll keep quiet about her for

the time being. See if she comes forward when we put out a general appeal."

And then he kissed her. A full, proper kiss, with tongues and his body pressing against hers. The effect was so strong that Jo swooned, would have fallen had he not been holding on to her, but she couldn't let that happen, no. So she'd pressed her feet into the ground, standing on tip-toe so that she could kiss him back properly before he broke away, and he'd let her, and the kiss had gone on for oh, minutes. He was the best kisser in the world. That smell – Calvin Klein, was it? – she would never forget. He smelt divine. If the world had ended later that night, Jo would have died happy.

And she couldn't tell a single girl at school about it, because not one of them would believe her. Worse, if she told them about the kiss, they wouldn't believe the rest of the story, about him walking with her to the restaurant. Truth was, most of them didn't believe that anyhow. What fan would forget to ask for an autograph?

When the kiss ended, they had pulled gently apart.

"I've got to go," he said.

"Yeah," was all she'd managed in reply.

"Come and see me again when you're sixteen," he told her, with that cheeky grin. He wiped his lips with a tissue, in case there was a lipstick smear, and went into the restaurant. She'd stood there for a moment, in a daze, then decided that it was uncool to hang about and walked hurriedly off, in the wrong direction, so that she didn't have to go past the restaurant, maybe see him with another woman.

"Now, here's a question that's very likely to come up in the SATs. Jo McCord, are you listening?"

"Yes. Sorry, Miss."

She answered the question on automatic, the main part of her brain wishing that she was nearly sixteen, not just turned fourteen. She wanted to know how Mark Murray knew her age when she could get served at some pubs in town, when the Year Eleven blokes she went out with insisted that Jo looked older than half the girls in their year. The reason, Jo reckoned, was this: Mark Murray really knew women. That kiss had proved it. So, when she *was* sixteen, she was going to find him. He had meant what he said. Mark was only twenty-two. What was eight years? Her dad was six years older than her mum. Jo would find him and…

The bell sounded. As she went to lunch, Jo passed Gemma Day, one of the unlucky girls who'd been waiting outside the Theatre Royal stage door two nights before. Gemma was in floods of tears.

"What's wrong?" Jo asked, convinced somehow that Gemma had found out that Jo had kissed her hero and was devastated by jealousy.

"Haven't you heard?" the girl with her asked, a girl who Jo didn't know.

"Heard what?"

"We just saw it on Ceefax in the library. It's Mark Murray. He's dead!"

5

"They're going to give it to me!" Curt announced, then began jumping up and down. "Fifty grand! Can you believe that? We're rich."

"Calm down," Julie told him, though she felt like leaping about herself. She'd been on this roller-coaster before, when Curt thought he had a winning lottery ticket. But, this time, it seemed, the story was for real. A tabloid newspaper had offered a fifty thousand pound reward for information leading to the return of a missing toddler. Curt had found the boy, returned him to the arms of his mother. Only trouble was, Curt had broken into the house where he'd found the little lad.

Ben, Julie's boyfriend, had played a blinder. He'd

presented a story to the press that Curt had broken in because he thought he heard something, and they, anxious to have good news for once, had bought it. Later, doubts surfaced, but not to pay Curt would have left the paper open to all kinds of embarrassment. A week after Social Services had threatened to take Curt into care, he was up for a bravery award. Best of all, as far as Julie was concerned, Ben's Inspector had dropped his objection to Ben and Julie living together. Before, her brother had been a little criminal whose mum had run off with a big criminal. After, Curt was a big hero.

So Ben had bitten the bullet. He'd given notice on his flat, moved in almost full time, and they were looking for something bigger. On top of that came the reward.

"Don't get too excited," Ben told him. "They're putting the money in trust until you're eighteen. All you'll get until then is the interest."

"How much?" Curt asked.

"Hard to say. Three thousand a year maybe."

"That's…" Curt paused. He wasn't too hot at maths.

"Sixty quid a week," Ben told him.

"Sixty quid a week! I'm rich!"

"Should keep you off crime, anyhow. Me and Julie might want you to pay something for your keep."

"Sod off!" Curt said, but there was a twinkle in

his eye, and Ben didn't seem to take the insult seriously.

"Shouldn't you be at school?" Ben commented. "I promised the social that we'd keep you going regular."

"On a day like today?"

"Even on a day like today. Yeah."

Ben scribbled a note apologizing for having kept Curt home because of "urgent family business". Julie had to pinch herself. They were a family. When Curt was gone, she put Tammy, her baby, down for a sleep, then snuggled up on the sofa with her boyfriend.

"Got time to go upstairs?"

"Don't see why not."

He was on afternoons this week, the shift she liked best. Lots of time to themselves. Before Ben, her mum had always been around: hard to have a proper relationship when Shirley could stick her head in at any minute. But Mum was gone for good. Julie was the lady of the house now. And Ben was her man.

Later, when he was showering before work, she put Radio Trent news on.

"Mark Murray, twenty-two-year-old TV and stage star has been found dead in a Nottingham hotel room. Murray missed last night's performance of the controversial play, *Selling England*. Police have not yet given the cause of death."

Drug overdose, Julie guessed, or suicide. How was it that people who had it all could throw away their lives like that? She used to watch Murray on the telly, half-fancied him. Before Tammy came along, when Julie went clubbing, you'd hear stories about the actor from girls who'd seen him in town. Some even claimed to have been with him. Always on the pull, they said. Liked them young, too. But Julie had never seen him around town, not once. And now she never would.

"Something wrong?"

Ben was out of the shower, reaching for a towel. Seeing him stopped Julie feeling maudlin. He was everything she'd ever wanted: tall, handsome, intelligent, muscular, his black skin glistening, god-like, as he dried himself.

"Nothing," she said. "How long have we got before you have to go?"

"Long enough," he said, dropping the towel as he reached for her.

Neil got to the Theatre Royal at one, just as the first mourners appeared. The midday news on Radio Nottingham had broken the story. They and the *Evening Post* had been told at eleven. This was thirty-five minutes before the *Post*'s deadline for its *City Final* edition, which was just hitting the streets. The front page read: "Mark Murray Murdered: police appeal for witnesses to his final hours."

Some girls had gone to the hotel where the actor had been killed, but the police had immediately shooed them away from the entrance. The Royal Centre complex had much more pavement outside for them to hold their vigil on. Neil had asked a uniform to talk to the girls. Maybe one of them would be the one who walked Mark to the restaurant the night before last. When you have no leads, check everything.

Inside the Theatre Royal, Neil was going over the list of free ticket users with the Theatre Royal's publicity officer.

"Who was meant to sit here?" he asked, pointing at a balcony seat which he had noticed was unoccupied.

"More press. Well, not proper press. The Trent University Students' Union paper. They got two tickets. Maybe they only used one. Actually, they were trying to set up an interview with the writer, but she wasn't in town for the production."

"Better give me the name of the reviewer," Neil said.

"Here it is. Peter Whiteside. The only number I've got is the uni one…" Neil took it. Glancing out of the window he saw Steve Garrett, the convicted thief who used to share a house with Clare. What on earth was he doing here?

"What's the writer's name? Trudy…"

"Runcible. Only twenty-seven. She got a best

first-play award for *Selling England* at the *Evening Standard* awards."

"Really," Neil said, unimpressed.

"The director's called Paul Santiago. He turned up yesterday. In fact, they're both around somewhere. I'll see if I can find them." Neil followed the publicity officer into the backstage belly of the theatre.

"I believe you're short an understudy," Steve said. "I got a call."

The director, distracted, didn't ask who the call came from, which was a good thing as there hadn't really been one. Steve had heard the news on the radio and came straight over. A chance like this only cropped up once in a lifetime.

"You know the play?" Paul Santiago asked.

"Saw it last night."

Paul, the director, turned to Trudy, the writer.

"He's got the right look," she said.

"I take it you've got an Equity card," Santiago said. Steve showed it to him.

"What've you done?"

Steve rattled off a list of his credits: Barker, Beckett, Brenton and Pinter, some of them non-existent productions to make him look more experienced than he was. Everybody faked their CV. It was expected.

"Impressive," Trudy Runcible said. "All right, give us a reading."

Paul handed him a script with Mark Murray's part marked. Steve felt his stomach flutter. This was his big chance. He hadn't seen Murray perform this part, but he could guess how he would do it. Should he imitate Murray? (After all, he was auditioning to be an understudy. But Murray was dead. Should he imitate Jeremy Eaton?) Best, he decided, just to be himself. He scanned the lines, then began.

You think I like doing this? You think I want it both ways when I could be with you all the time? All I want is you.

Then have me then – Trudy read out.

But what do we live on? Tell me that. If I stop, there's one thing I want to know...

"Sorry to interrupt," a familiar voice said. "But I need a word with Ms Runcible and Mr Santiago." The detective who used to go out with Clare led them both away.

"I'll get back to you," the director told Steve, a phrase which meant the same as *don't call us, we'll call you*. "Leave your number at the door."

"Auditioning for a replacement?" Neil asked, as Steve left.

"Understudy," Paul Santiago told him. "Jeremy will take over Mark's part for the rest of the tour."

Was that enough of a motive for murder? Neil wondered. A stab at fame?

"Were he and Mark friends?" he asked.

"Mark didn't have many male friends," Trudy

told him. "Oh, maybe here, in Nottingham. But Mark was a ladies' man."

"So I gathered," Neil said. He was fed up with people telling him that Mark Murray was some kind of a sex god. "Did you get on with him?" he asked.

"Sure. Actors have to try and get on with directors." Neil sensed an undercurrent of distaste.

"But you didn't like each other?"

Santiago shrugged. "If I'm honest, no. Mark wasn't a great actor. He was a pretty face who we used to get bums on seats in the provinces. Mark probably knew that I'd never have cast him for a London production." *What a snob*, Neil thought, but didn't say.

"But there was something in it for him too, presumably?"

"Oh, yes. Credibility. He wanted to get into films, but would never make it on the back of two years in a soap and bit parts here and there. It looked like his tactics were working, too. Trudy ... you tell the story."

The writer looked embarrassed. "It wasn't definite."

"Yeah, but, tell him."

"Leo Fitzgerald, a big name cinema director, was interested in filming *Selling England*. He was considering Mark for the lead part. Ironically, he came to see him in the role last night."

And got to see Jeremy Eaton instead, Neil thought. Interesting.

"Is Fitzgerald still around?" he asked.

"Leo didn't stay to watch the whole play," Paul Santiago told him.

"So nobody told him what had happened to Mark?"

"We didn't know ourselves. The hotel weren't allowed to tell the company that Mark was dead, only that he was indisposed. And Mark has ... had a bit of a reputation. Fitzgerald jumped to a conclusion, as we all did, and left after the first half. Look, I promised Jeremy we'd go over some scenes with him."

"That's all right," Neil said. "I'll talk to Ms Runcible first."

"Jeremy needs her there, too. There are some issues of interpretation."

"I won't keep her long, I promise."

The director left Neil alone in the room with the writer. Trudy Runcible was a tall, striking woman, with a shock of frizzy, red hair. Her face was spoiled by what resembled a boxer's broken nose, with a gold stud through it. Neil wondered why she didn't have a nose job: some kind of feminist thing, maybe. Clare would know.

"How about you?" he asked. "Did you get on with Mark Murray?"

"So-so. I didn't object to his casting, if that's what you want to know."

"But you weren't too happy with it?"

"There were one or two people who I would have preferred, but, like Paul said, touring the provinces is about bums on seats. Mark brought in an audience."

"Were you and he … friendly?" Trudy smiled. "Yes, but he never tried it on with me, if that's what you're getting at. He was one of those guys who're intimidated by intelligent women." Neil knew what she meant, though he was the opposite: drawn to women who were cleverer than him: Clare, Melanie…

"Mark knew that I was with Anna anyhow."

"Anna Anyhow?"

"Anna Derbyshire. She plays Stella in *Selling England*. We live together."

"Oh, right." Acting must be the same as everything else, Neil thought: not what you know but who you know, who you've slept with.

"That didn't stop him making a pass at Anna," Neil pointed out, and Trudy gave him a funny look. Had she known? Trudy wasn't that attractive, as far as Neil was concerned. Maybe that was why Mark hadn't made a pass at her. And maybe Anna Derbyshire was with Trudy in order to further her career. Maybe, despite what she'd told Neil the night before, Anna preferred men. Maybe she hadn't turned Mark down. In a case like this, all the courses said, trust nobody.

He stopped speculating and asked the playwright one final question.

"Just a formality, but … can you tell me where you were between four and seven yesterday evening?"

"Yes, I was at the Royal Court rehearsal space in Soho, workshopping my second play. There are about fifteen people who can vouch for me. We broke up at about five, I think."

That wouldn't allow her to get to Nottingham by seven, which was the latest time that the murder could have taken place.

"OK," said Neil. "Thanks. That'll be all for now."

"Good luck," Trudy said, holding out her hand. "I hope that you catch whoever did it."

"So do I," Neil said.

Her handshake was firm, almost aggressive. Neil made a note to himself to watch her play that night. You never knew: it might give him an idea or two.

After questioning Paul Santiago, who had been with Leo Fitzgerald at the relevant times, Neil asked the director whether there was any chance of a free ticket.

"Sure, I'll leave your name at the box office. Want to bring a friend?"

"Maybe."

"All right. That's Neil Foster plus one."

Santiago made a note. "You don't think that you'll find a clue to who did this in the play, d'you? Like some cheesy whodunnit? Because it's not that kind of play."

"I don't know what to expect," Neil said. "We're checking everything."

"I hope you and your friend aren't too easily shocked," Santiago said.

"No," Neil promised. "We're not."

He rang Melanie when he got back to the station. It was nearly knocking off time.

"Hello stranger," she said. It had been a week since he'd seen her. She'd had coursework to finish. He'd been on overtime.

"I wondered if you were doing anything tonight."

"Nothing I can't put aside for you," she replied. "Got anything in mind?"

"It's a little creepy," Neil said.

"Now you've got me really interested…" she said, flirtatiously.

"It's to do with this murder I'm investigating. I've got two tickets for the play that Mark Murray was in. Would you like to come?" Melanie went quiet on him. "Something wrong?"

"No, no, I was just thinking … you're right. It's a little creepy. Do you mind if I pass, Neil? I really don't like getting involved with your work."

"OK. But I've got to go. Shall we do something tomorrow night instead?"

"I've arranged to meet some people. But I'm seeing you Saturday anyway."

"OK. Until then." He put the phone down, wondering who else might accompany him. Clare? But she had seen the play already. He rang Ben, then remembered that he was on duty until ten. Still, he got the answering-machine message.

"If I'm not here, you can often find me on..." Neil recognized the digits at the beginning of the number. Somewhere in the Meadows. Had Ben moved in with Julie Wilder? No wonder he saw so little of his friend these days. Who else could he take? No one sprang to mind. Maybe he'd have to go on his own.

6

By the time Clare's taxi arrived, Kathy Murray had settled in and was having a bath.

"You don't have to go," Mum said. "Kathy could have Angelo's room."

"I don't think so, Mum." Her brother had been dead for two and a half years. His room had been cleared a while back. But it was never used.

The house that Clare shared with Sam, Ruth and Gary was only half a mile away. The taxi driver was disappointed by the smallness of the fare. He didn't help Clare to haul her three bags out of his cab and into the hall. Steve and Sam were in the kitchen. The landlady's boyfriend helped Clare to carry her stuff upstairs.

"Why're you moving back now?" he asked her.

"I'm off my stick, back at work," she said, not wanting to tell him about Kathy Murray. Steve was the sort of bloke who, when short of money, might sell the address to a tabloid.

"Glad to hear it." He went back down and told Sam that he'd better get back to his flat. "Just in case." *Just in case* what? Clare wondered, but didn't ask.

Sam and Clare hadn't seen each other for a while. The two women were friendly, but not close. Sam offered to show Clare the photos from her holiday in Tunisia.

"Another time," Clare said. "I'm meant to be on duty." She wondered if DI Greasby had told her boss, Inspector Winter, that she was working with him. Best not to bring it up, she thought, in case Winter threw a wobbly. The Inspector had barely been in the post a week when she went off sick. Clare hardly knew the man. When she got to the station, she mentioned her situation to DI Greasby.

"I'll sort it with Tony Winter, don't you worry. Now, tell me, did you get any more information from Kathy Murray while you were moving her over to your mum's?"

"Not really. She seems convinced that it was a jealous bloke."

Kathy had given Clare the names of a string of girlfriends from Mark's Nottingham days. Some had surnames. A handful had addresses. Most were first names with flimsy descriptions: less than useless. Also, Kathy was unlikely to know about the one-night stands or married women who Mark was seeing on the side.

From what Kathy said, Mark had only had two really serious girlfriends before leaving Nottingham. First, Janine Taylor, who would be twenty-one now, a year younger than Mark. They had a long relationship while Mark was in the sixth-form. Then there was Gill Crane, who came from out of town, Kathy wasn't sure where, and had met Mark on their *Next Stage* drama course. They had been together "on and off" Kathy said (which probably meant that Mark cheated on her half the time) for at least six months.

"Why don't I start by trying to track down these two?" Clare suggested, and Greasby agreed.

"But if you happen to get lucky and one of them answers the phone, don't do an interview. Just ask them to come into the station as soon as they can. OK?"

"OK," Clare said, happy to be involved in detective work rather than pounding a beat, even if she was back to being CID's dogsbody again.

"Look at this in the paper," Lisa Kelly said during the first lesson of the afternoon. "The police are appealing to witnesses who saw Mark during his three days in Nottingham, even if they don't think that they saw anything suspicious. That's you, Jo!" It was a wind up, Jo knew that. Lisa didn't think that Jo had spent some time with Mark Murray. Well, her moments with him had been precious, and private. She wasn't telling.

"Ooh, look. They particularly want to trace a woman who he had dinner with on Tuesday night. You didn't tell us that he took you for a meal, Jo!" Jo wished that she hadn't gone back to school, that she'd stayed with the other girls at the vigil outside the theatre. But Jo wasn't a skiver. She didn't like getting into trouble. She'd already skipped the lesson before lunch. Skipping afternoon school wouldn't bring Mark back.

"Something wrong, Jo?" Ms Clumber asked. "You look very pale."

"She's been crying 'cos that actor died, Miss," some idiot called out.

"I know how you feel, Jo," the teacher said. "I rather liked Mark Murray myself." That caused general hilarity in the maths class.

"Well, I can dream, can't I?" the teacher, who was nearly *thirty*, protested. Nobody understood. Nobody would ever understand Jo now that Mark was gone. Fourteen years old and her life was over.

Who was the woman who Mark was having dinner with the other night? Jo hadn't even seen her. So there was no point in her going to the police, was there.

*   *   *

At the Theatre Royal, Neil reinterviewed the security man who had seen Mark Murray leaving the theatre with a teenage girl on Tuesday night.

"How old did you reckon?" was the first question.

"Seventeen or so."

"Do you have children that age yourself?"

"No kids, me."

"That girl over there," Neil said, pointing at one of the kids on the vigil for Mark Murray. "How old would you say?"

"Sixteen." Neil nodded. The girl was fourteen, at most. He was used to the way that girls could make themselves look older. This guy wasn't.

"And the girl you saw was a bit older, blonde?"

"S'right." Neil pressed the guy for a more detailed description but got nothing more. Best guess, he decided, was fifteen. Had Murray arranged to meet the girl later? Was that why he had ducked out of his dinner date early?

"Bloke on the phone for you," Clare said, as Neil walked in to the incident room. "Peter something. From the university newspaper."

"Oh, right. Good." Neil took it from her, and explained to Peter Whiteside why he was calling. "There was an empty seat next to you. We need to establish why. Did you only use one of your two review tickets?"

"No, it wasn't that," Whiteside said. "I took a date, but she felt ill and left as soon as the interval began. I had to stay because I was reviewing it."

"Fair enough," Neil said. "Can I have her name and address, please, for our records?"

"Sure. Her name's Melanie Byatt. She's got a flat on Wellington Square, in Lenton. The flat's number 'c' but I can't remember the number of the house, sorry. Hello? Hello?"

"Are you all right, Neil?" Clare asked, spotting his reddening face.

"Yeah, uh … yeah. Hold on." Neil's mind had gone into overdrive. He took a deep breath. "Sorry," he said. "I was interrupted. You say this is your girlfriend, but you don't know the number of the house she lives in?"

"I've only just started seeing her," Whiteside said. "I'm meeting her for coffee in a few minutes. I can call you back with her address, if it's really that important."

"No, no, not important at all," Neil said. Would Whiteside tell Melanie he'd been talking to Neil? Had Neil given him his full name? Would this bloke remember it? "Thanks for your cooperation," he said, and hung up.

"Is something wrong?" Clare asked. They were alone in the incident room. Had anyone else asked, Neil would have lied. That was the culture. But this was Clare.

"What is it?" she said, coming close to him, so close that he could smell the Issey Miyake perfume she always used.

"It's Melanie," he said. "She's two-timing me."

He explained the situation to Clare.

"She must have seen me in the interval, looking around, and made up that being sick story so that she could leave before I spotted her."

"It sounds like you're making too much of it," Clare said. "This guy had a free ticket. Melanie does the odd review for the university paper, you've told me that before. She went along too. Doesn't mean that she's interested in him."

"He called it a *date*."

"Doesn't mean that she thought of it as one. Men's perceptions of how they stand with women are often radically different from what the woman thinks."

"He said he was having coffee with her in a few minutes."

"He's the Arts editor of the university paper, right?"

"Right. And Melanie's two-timing me with him."

"Or she could be doing an article for him. Go over and see her tonight. She told you she was free. Sort it out."

"I'm meant to be going to the play," Neil protested.

"Do it another night."

"She lied to me. She didn't tell me that she'd already seen it."

"That's not exactly a lie," Clare pointed out.

"No," Neil said. "I suppose it isn't." But he was on the way out of her life. He could feel it.

Clare watched Neil start to crumble. What else could she say? She was the worst person for him to talk to, having hurt him badly six months ago, when she refused to marry him. Her phone rang, saving her from the decision. It was Janine Taylor's mother. Clare had left a message on her answering machine.

"We understand that your daughter used to go out with Mark Murray," Clare said. "We're interviewing all of his close friends and former friends. Tell me, does she still live with you?"

"Yes, yes. Janine's very upset, as you might imagine."

"Would it be possible for you to bring her in this afternoon for an interview? We need to follow up every angle as quickly as possible."

"I suppose so. In about an hour?"

"Thank you. DS Dylan will see you."

Next, Clare ran a PNC check on Gillian Crane, using her last known address in Sneinton. The results were surprising. Gill Crane had been reported missing nearly eighteen months ago. Finding her had not been a police priority: Gill was an adult. She would be twenty two now. Clare made a note to do a full check with social security and other institutions when they were open again the following morning.

When Clare looked up, Neil had gone, for which she was grateful. No more words of comfort came to mind. It sounded like Melanie was running two blokes at once, a pretty easy thing to do if you were a university student and bloke number one was a police officer working all hours.

Across the room, DI Greasby was taking a phone call. Clare didn't know what the call was about, but Greasby looked excited. He kept saying things like "really" and "are you sure" and concluded with "we'll be right there".

"Where the hell's Neil?" Greasby asked, as he put down the phone.

"Personal time," Clare said.

"And Dylan?"

"Sorting out an interview room. Janine Taylor – one of Murray's exes – is on her way in."

"I can't interview this girl alone," the DI told her. "You'd better come with me."

"What's it about?"

"That was Dan Rossiter at the *Evening Post*."

"Have they found the woman who had dinner with Mark?"

"Better than that," Greasby said. "They've got a teenage girl who's confessed to killing him!"

7

Melanie's flat was on the third floor of a Victorian terrace at the highest point of Derby Road, a hill which descended to the city centre on one side and the old university on the other. Neil's girlfriend went to Trent, the new university, which was based in the city centre and on a campus in Clifton, a few miles out of town. She should be home soon, unless she was still having coffee with Peter Whiteside.

Technically, Neil was still on duty, but if he went to the play tonight, he would be doing unpaid overtime, so could justify an hour off in lieu. He didn't know what he hoped to learn from the play but, so far, the investigation seemed to be going nowhere. If a murder wasn't solved (which isn't the same as *proved*) in the first three days, then CID were in for a long, hard slog with little likelihood of a result. Today, twenty-four hours after the event, some lateral thinking might come in useful. But Neil's thinking at the moment was anything but lateral.

He and Melanie had been together for six months. Neil wasn't looking for a girlfriend when he met her. He'd only just broken up with Clare. No, tell a lie: it was just before Clare dumped him. First, he'd investigated a burglary in Melanie's hall of residence. Then he'd bumped into her on a hot night in late May, given her a lift to a party. Much to his amazement, the gorgeous Melanie came on to him. He'd announced, primly, that he had a girl-friend. She'd told him not to flatter himself that she was interested. Later, though, Mel admitted she'd fancied him from the start, and was delighted when, soon afterwards, she learnt that Clare was out of the picture.

But there'd been a darker side to their relation-ship, too. Two girls from her hall had been raped. Melanie was nearly the rapist's next victim. Almost as soon as Neil and Melanie started sleeping together, they began living together. Melanie had been anxious to get out of the hall where horrible things had happened. Their relationship, as a result, became too intense too quickly. A month ago, to Neil's dismay, Melanie got her own flat. She said that her leaving had nothing to do with the way she felt about him. Yet, inevitably, they'd seen less of each other since.

Was Clare right? Was Peter Whiteside only showing off about Melanie, claiming to have a girl-friend when he was talking to an anonymous copper on the phone? Men made up stories about their exploits with women all the time. Chris Dylan, for instance, was all hints and innuendo. You were never certain how much was true, how much mere self-aggrandizement. Neil himself never felt the need to show off (though he had never corrected the male officers who nudgingly assumed that he was sleeping with Clare, when he wasn't).

Neil couldn't believe his luck when he got off with Melanie, by far the best looking woman he'd ever been with. There were times when, in bed with her, he had to pinch himself to make sure that it was real. She certainly didn't look real now, walking into Wellington Square, too preoccupied to notice Neil's old Cortina. She looked like Neil's worst nightmare.

For Melanie was with another guy. A long haired, bearded, bohemian. Neil watched as she opened the front door of her house, and he closed it behind both of them. In anguish, Neil stared up at her bedroom window, waiting to see if they pulled the blind down.

The *Evening Post* used to be based in a block of its own, a piece of prime real estate opposite the Royal

Concert Hall. Now it had a brand new glass castle between the canal and the city centre. Clare and Greasby weren't allowed through security. They had to wait for Rossiter to come down and meet them.

"He's on the phone I'm afraid," the silver haired guard told them. "If you don't mind waiting…" Impatiently, Greasby picked at his fingernails. A disgusting habit, Clare thought, but the DI was her boss and seemingly unaware of what he was doing. She spent her time thinking about the girl they were about to see. What kind of teenage girl had it in her to kill a grown man?

"Still on the phone," the security guard apologized.

"This girl who came in," Greasby said to him "Did she see you first?"

"S'right. Asked for Dan Rossiter. I'll tell you, five minutes later, the place went mad. Photographers all over the place. Reporters called in from holiday. Whatever she's got, it must be a big story…"

"Try the number again," Greasby said. He did. "Still engaged."

"What time did she come in?" Clare asked.

"Can't say for sure."

"But you made her sign in?"

"That's right, yes."

"Check the log, please," Greasby said.

"I suppose that'll be all right." He looked through

a black ledger. "Here we are. Tamara Crane. Three twenty-two."

"*What?*" It was now five to five. Greasby turned to Clare, his face burning.

"They've had her here for an hour and a half. When I get my hands on…"

"Sorry," the security man said, putting the phone down again. "Still engaged."

"Look," Greasby said, nearly grabbing the guy by the scruff of his neck, although he was old enough to be Clare's grandfather. "This is a murder investigation and you've got a prime suspect in there. I want to be shown in *now*! Understand me?"

"Yes, sir."

The security man tried the phone again. "It's ringing. He muttered a few words then turned to Greasby with a smug smile. "He'll be with you in a moment, Sir."

Rossiter joined them two minutes later. "Sorry for the delay," he said. "It's mad in here today. First the murder, then the confession."

"You've had this girl for an hour and half?" Greasby complained.

"We had to check her story out," Rossiter told him. "At first we thought that she was a nutter." They would say that, wouldn't they? Clare thought. Fake or genuine, the confession would make front page news tomorrow.

"What's she like?" Greasby wanted to know.

"Quite tasty, if you like them young. A bit hysterical at first, but she's calmed down now."

"Taken a few photos, have you?"

"Yes. Look, Detective Inspector, we both know the score, don't we? The girl came in, asked to speak to me. When she'd said what she had to say I told Duncan, our Crime Correspondent. He put a team together to check her out."

"Getting to witnesses before us," Greasby sneered. "Not very helpful to police procedure."

"Or, to put it another way, saving you valuable police hours."

"Giving her time to get her story straight…"

"She's confessing, for chrissake!"

This discussion was going nowhere, Clare thought. Press and police relied on each other. No serious falling out was in prospect. By now they had walked to the newsroom, a sea of computers, phones, stacked files and highbacked swivel chairs.

"Where is she?" Greasby asked.

"A room in editorial with one of our girls. In the old days we'd have locked her in or put a security guard on the door. Still, I don't think she's gonna run."

"Detective Inspector!" A bespectacled bloke with a Walt Disney tie stood up to greet Greasby and Clare. She'd seen him around: Duncan Smith, the *Post*'s crime correspondent.

"We might have a fast result for you," Smith told

Greasby. "This girl's story checks out. She definitely knows ... I mean, *knew* Murray. The mother confirms that. He used to go out with her elder sister. And she's got a motive. Seems Murray screwed up her sister's life."

"Murder weapon?" Greasby asked. Nothing had been recovered from the hotel room.

"A brass statuette brought along for the purpose. Says she ditched it in the Trent."

"And why on earth did she come here and confess?"

"That's two questions," Smith replied. "*Why did she confess?* Dunno. She's not ashamed of what she did, I'll tell you that. *Why did she come here?* Easy. She wants us to tell the world what a creep Mark Murray was, why he deserved to die."

"All right," said Greasby. "Take us to her."

Smith hesitated. "First things first. No giving the story to other media until our first edition's on the street."

"I'm not making any promises," Greasby said. "You'll get a news blackout if it's appropriate."

Smith scratched his head. "Not sure I can remember what room she's in, now I come to think of it..."

"All right, all right," Greasby said, balling the fingers of both hands into fists. "No press conference until midday tomorrow, presuming that we make an arrest and the super has no objections."

"The super better not have any objections," Smith replied, as they reached the door to the editor's office. "She's in here."

whether ... the ... ...

... ...

8

Tamara Crane was tall and blonde, with long straight hair and a tight, V-necked top. Clare wondered whether it was hers or if someone on the *Post* had lent it to her to be photographed in. She matched the description of the girl seen outside the Theatre Royal, the one who walked Murray to the restaurant. When she opened her mouth, Tamara's accent was east country, not Nottingham.

"I suppose I have to answer all those questions all over again."

"You certainly do," DI Greasby said. "Back at the station. But I'd like to clear up a few things first. How did you know Mark Murray?"

She crossed and uncrossed her legs. "Met him when my sister was going out with him. She was twenty then. I was fifteen. He came to visit us in Norwich once."

"The mother confirmed that," Dan Rossiter said. "I phoned her earlier."

"All right, thank you," Greasby told him. "How did you get into his room?" Tamara pouted. "That's for me to know and you to find out."

"Was Mark Murray expecting you to be there?"

"Maybe."

"You'd seen him earlier in the day?"

"S'right. Outside Radio Trent."

"And you walked with him back to his hotel?"

"No." That was good. Several witnesses said that they'd seen Murray walking back alone.

"You met him at the hotel?"

"Yes."

"Did you sleep with him?" She hesitated. At this stage, the police didn't know whether Mark Murray had had sex before he died. The autopsy wasn't in.

"I took my clothes off," she said, slowly.

"And?" Greasby asked. "Did he undress too?" Murray had been fully clothed when found, but this hadn't been reported, not yet.

"I took my clothes off so that I wouldn't get any blood on me, so there wouldn't be any evidence. But I didn't let him touch me."

"Yet you're confessing now," Greasby said. "Why?"

"I've seen the news all afternoon, making him out to be a wonderful person."

Greasby took a deep breath. "So why did you do it, Tamara?" he asked.

"Revenge," she said.

One thing Chris Dylan could say about Mark Murray: he had good taste in women. Janine Taylor was the girl he'd dated when he was in the sixth-form. She had a trim, womanly figure and fine brown hair, expensively styled. She did not, despite what her mother had told Clare earlier, seem too shattered by the actor's death.

"When did you last see Mark?" he asked.

"Apart from on TV? Three years ago. He was on this drama course. I bumped into him on the street and he was going on about how great it was, so I went to see him in a play at College Street and went for a drink afterwards. It was summer. We sat out-side the Playhouse bar. But there was another girl there. One of the actresses from the play. Mark was all over her. I think he only wanted me there to show off to this girl, make it clear that she wasn't the only one interested."

"He was insecure about his looks?" Dylan asked.

"Mark wasn't famous then. He was just another bloke with spots and a bad haircut. And, on the evidence of that play, he wasn't a very good actor, either."

"Remember the other girl's name?"

"No. I'm not sure if I could even describe her." Dylan pulled out a photo of Gill Crane which had been supplied by Murray's mother. "Is this her?"

"Maybe." She hesitated. "Yes, probably. But I can't be absolutely certain."

"How did you feel about Mark? Resentful?"

"Because he dumped me? No. Our break-up was mutual. He wanted to play the field and I was growing up. I wanted someone with more depth." *Depth*, Dylan thought. What the hell did that mean? Probably rules me out, anyway.

"He cheated on you when you were going out with each other?" Janine hesitated, then shrugged before replying, as if to imply that this was a past life that she was talking about.

"He cheated on me with half of my friends, as it turned out. Not that I knew at the time, or I'd have shown him his cards. But once we were through, people started to tell me. Nights when I was home doing schoolwork he was out with her, or her. A couple of them apologized to me – he was so persistent, they said, so full of himself, so *charming*. See, he was my first – you know – I didn't know that that was what some blokes did. Better to learn the lesson at sixteen than after you've married the sod, I suppose."

"So you did harbour a grudge against Murray?" Chris probed.

"Life's too short," Janine told him. "We parted friends. I've been hurt worse by other blokes since."

"Were you upset when you heard that he was dead?" Dylan asked, then was annoyed with himself. *How did you feel* was how the question should have begun.

"Of course I was," Janine replied, shortly. "Am. Yes." She looked at Dylan, could see what he was thinking: you don't *look* upset.

"But not devastated," she added. "Like I said, I'm long over him."

"Just for the record, could you tell me where you were between four and seven yesterday evening?"

"Sure. My last lecture finished at five. I walked home. We live in Wollaton. It's only a twenty minute walk back from the uni, so I must have got back before half past. Mum got in from work at a quarter to six, Dad at about his usual time, ten past maybe. So they can vouch for ... or whatever you call it ... alibi me."

"Fine, thanks." Dylan gave her his card. "If you think of anything else that might be relevant. Call me." Janine smiled graciously, a smile which showed that she wouldn't be calling him for any other reason. "I hope you catch whoever did this," she said.

Dylan saw her out the back way, but still had to fend off several journalists as the girl got into her mother's car. A photographer on a motorbike followed the car out. Doubtless Janine would be selling her story to the papers. There was nothing Chris could do to stop her. Soon, he suspected, everybody's evidence would be corrupted by the media. The more salacious you made the story, the more you could sell it for. Truth didn't enter into the equation.

There was a whiteboard in the incident room. On it, Greasby had written a list of former lovers and possible suspects in the Mark Murray killing. Janine Taylor was at the top. Doubtful now, Dylan thought, but he left it there. Next came Gill Crane. They hadn't tracked her down yet. She had done a drama course, but wasn't registered with Equity, so presumably hadn't made it as an actor, yet.

Then came people from the Royal Court Theatre: Lynda Crabbe was first, for she had slept with Murray and had a relatively flimsy alibi for the time of his death (Dylan reminded himself to go to the Odeon, see if anyone had seen her leave the film. Lynda could have bought a ticket but never gone in).

Anna Derbyshire was up there, as was Trudy Runcible, whose alibi had yet to be confirmed. But they had no apparent motive or opportunity. Then there were the men: Paul Santiago, the director, had been with Leo Fitzgerald during the relevant hours. He could, theoretically, have slipped away to kill

Murray, though Dylan didn't believe that for a moment. Jeremy Eaton, on the other hand, had a motive. He was the understudy who got to take over the main role. Dylan hadn't met Eaton, but his alibi was non-existent. He had to be a prospect.

Who did that leave? Dylan added two unnamed people to the list: the teenage girl who'd walked Murray to the restaurant, and the woman he'd met there. Finally, there was the possibility of a jealous husband – or any number of jealous husbands.

When he'd finished, the list looked like this:

SUSPECTS

Janine Taylor
Gill Crane
Trudy Runcible
Anna Derbyshire
Lynda Crabbe
Girl outside restaurant
Woman in restaurant

Paul Santiago
Jeremy Eaton
Jealous husband?

Neil came in and admired his handiwork.

"This Jeremy Eaton," Dylan said. "What do you make of him as a suspect?"

"Didn't look like a murderer to me," Neil said. "But what do I know? I'm going to the play tonight, see if it gives me any ideas. There's a spare ticket if you want to tag along."

"All right," Dylan said. "Why not? Know where the DI is?"

"Someone said something about him going over to the *Evening Post* building. Don't know why."

The two men arranged to meet at the Theatre Royal at seven-fifty, then signed out. Neil looked distracted, Chris thought. Where'd he just been?

They got Tamara Crane to the station at ten past six, making sure that the back entrance was cleared of media first. Detective Superintendent Petit turned up to take a look at her.

"Has the Crane girl asked for a solicitor?" The DS wanted to know.

"No, Ma'am," Greasby told her. "She just wants to get it off her chest. I've sent for the witnesses who saw the suspect. There're two young women who were standing outside Radio Trent. Then there's Penelope Palmer from Stokely's restaurant. She saw Tamara snogging Murray."

"Tamara hasn't said that she was the girl outside the restaurant," Clare pointed out.

"There's a lot she hasn't said," Greasby agreed. "Which is why she's only helping us with our enquiries. Arrest her and it'll be splashed all over the media. If she's only an attention seeker, there'd be egg on all our faces."

"If she's an attention seeking fake," DS Petit said, "she shouldn't be hard to catch out. I'll leave you to it."

"What other angles are you pursuing, Ma'am?" Clare asked. The DS gave her a *who-the-hell-are-you?* look.

"Concentrate on one thing at a time," she told her. There was no official line on Mark Murray's death. The local paper's only guess was that he had interrupted a burglary. A team from Major Crimes, under DS Petit, were checking the alibis of known thieves who preyed on hotels.

"The *Post* goes to press at eight thirty-five tomorrow morning," the DS reminded Greasby. "Perhaps you could decide whether to charge her by then."

"I can't stop them looking stupid if they're wrong, or claiming the glory if they're right," Greasby complained to Clare once the DS was gone. "But if we're going to charge her, I agree with the DS. It would be politic to do it in the morning, then call a press conference before the paper hits the streets. Otherwise we're going to have a lot of angry people from every other paper, TV and Radio station. Weren't planning an early night tonight, were you?"

"No, Sir," Clare said.

"Come on, then. Let's see if we can get to the bottom of this."

9

"There was this girl at school today," Natalie told Julie, "claims she met Mark Murray on Tuesday night."

"The night before he died?"

"Yeah. Jo McCord, her name is. Says she was hanging around the back door at the Theatre Royal when he came out. He wanted to know where this restaurant was, so she showed him. 'Course, nobody believes her."

"Why not?" Julie asked, spooning spaghetti hoops on to brown toast. Natalie, her brother's girl-friend, came round for dinner once a week.

"She didn't get his autograph, did she? How could you meet Mark Murray and not get his autograph?"

"Some people think that autographs are stupid. Did she talk to him?"

"For ten minutes, she says."

"That's much more impressive – having a conversation with him – that's making a real connection."

"S'pose," Natalie said. "She's not the sort of person who makes things up, Jo isn't. And she did say that he was meeting some woman in the restaurant. That was before it was in the paper or on the telly."

"There you go, then."

The police were appealing for this woman to come forward in order to eliminate her from their enquiries. Though Julie didn't see why they needed her, not if the actor's death was a burglary which went wrong. He was single and he was seeing someone. So what?

"Has she gone to the police, this girl?" The police were also appealing for anybody who'd seen Mark in the last twenty-four hours of his life to come forward.

"Jo? Go to the police?" Natalie sneered. "I hope she's got more sense. What's on telly tonight?" Julie threw the paper at her. She'd nearly finished it, and wasn't interested in the story she'd just started reading. *Top City Lawyer To Wed For Second Time*. She hardly took in the picture of the middle-aged white man with a beautiful young black woman, neither of whom she'd ever met. By the time that Ben came home, the paper would be in the bin.

"See the news today?"

Dylan had joined Neil in the Theatre Royal foyer, where Neil was queueing to collect their tickets for the night's performance. It was a big queue. Most of the people in front of them seemed to be asking for refunds, with no joy.

"About Murray?" Neil asked.

"Nah. About your friend Ben's ex, what's her name?"

"Ruth?"

"No, the black one."

"Charlene … her surname's Harris, I think."

"Not for much longer," Dylan told him. "She's marrying her boss. Jagger and Jagger, that's what the firm'll be called."

"But he's…" Neil was confused. Charlene and Jagger? Surely not.

"Old enough to be her dad, and then some. I know."

"God," Neil said, his mind lifting from his own problems for a moment. "Ben'll be…"

"I certainly wouldn't want to be the one to tell him," Dylan commented.

"You say it was in the paper?"

"Towards the back."

"What do you know about Jagger?" Neil asked. Ben had a thing about the city lawyer, which would make Charlene's marriage twice as hurtful.

"Jagger?" Dylan rolled his eyes. "I wouldn't trust any lawyer as far as I could throw him. But he's well connected, everyone knows that."

They had reached the front of the queue. The tickets were waiting: the front row of the circle. Attached to them was a note from the director, Paul Santiago: *There's something you ought to know. Could you come backstage after the performance?*

Tamara Crane had not asked for a solicitor, but her mother had come over from Norwich and was waiting to speak to her at the police's convenience. Mrs Crane had been alerted by the *Evening Post*, rather than Tamara herself.

"All right," Greasby said, as the tapes rolled. "Let's go over this one more time. Murray dumped your sister and ruined her life. Three months later, she vanished. You're pretty certain that she killed herself, though no body's ever been found and she didn't send a note. So you decided to murder Murray in return, as revenge for what he did to Gill. You chatted him up outside Radio Trent, got his room number, then went back to his hotel and waited for him, naked. As soon as he came into the room, you killed him with a sharp blow to the head with a blunt instrument, namely a brass statuette which you bought in an antiques shop and which you later deposited in the River Trent."

"That's it, yes."

"How did you get into his room?" Greasby.

"Magic." Clever little cow, Clare thought. "Where did you buy the statuette?" she asked.

"A shop on the Derby Road," Tamara told them. "I don't remember which." There were several antiques shops on Derby Road.

"Yesterday?" Greasby.

"No. On Monday. I came on Monday."

"So why did you wait until Wednesday?" Greasby wanted to know.

"It was my first chance."

"Did you see him on Tuesday night, too?" Clare.

"Yes, but I didn't get to talk to him."

"So you didn't walk with him to a restaurant?" Clare again.

"No."

"The first time that you talked to him was on Wednesday afternoon, outside Radio Trent?" Greasby.

"Yes."

"Would you be willing for a couple of people to take a look at you, confirm that they saw you there?" Greasby suggested.

"Of course."

"All right," Greasby said. "We'll do that, then we'll let you see your mother."

"I don't want to see Mum!" Clare glanced at her in surprise. If she'd just confessed to murder, she'd want to see *her* mother.

"Just stay where you are," Greasby said. "Clare, do the honours." Clare went and found the security man from the Theatre Royal. They didn't have any of the girls who'd been outside Radio Trent, as none of them had come forward. But there was no need to tell Tamara that they were actually checking a different part of her story.

"I shouldn't be here, you know," the bloke said. "The curtain's just gone up."

"It'll only take a moment," Clare promised. She led him to the glass-fronted interview room.

"Is that the girl who you saw on Tuesday night, the one who showed Murray the way to the restaurant?" The man stared long and hard. "Could be. I can't be sure. Hair's right, but I thought she were a bit … younger. Dunno."

Clare wasn't surprised. When they'd called in the doorman and Penelope, the restaurant's co-owner, the police had assumed that Tamara was the girl from that night, the one he'd kissed. Tamara had hinted as much earlier. But now she said she wasn't.

Penelope Palmer couldn't say one way or another. Tamora's photo was "like her, but a bit too old," she said.

Clare met with Greasby in the incident room.

"What do you reckon?" he said.

"Her story checks out so far."

"I'm uncertain," Greasby told her. "There's no evidence whatsoever apart from her confession. I'm going to ring DS Petit, see if she reckons we ought to charge Tamara based on the confession alone. Then, tomorrow, we hit the antiques shops, put out an appeal for anyone who saw her in the hotel or outside Radio Trent. The paper's bound to splash her photo all over its first three pages whether we charge her or not. So we might as well turn that to our advantage."

"But what's your gut feeling, Sir?" Clare asked.

Greasby hesitated. "I don't have one. She could have done it, but I'm nowhere near convinced. You?" Clare considered for a moment before replying.

"I don't know why, but I think she's making it up."

It wasn't just Mark Murray who was missing from that night's performance of *Selling England*. Anna Derbyshire had been replaced by Lynda Crabbe, who, in Neil's book, was a rather less enticing prospect. The play's story reminded him of the job: pimps and blackmail, drugs and deceit. Nobody trusted anybody and love was a commodity like any other, inseparable from sex.

The playwright, he read in the programme, was meant to speak for her generation, "telling it like it is". Maybe Trudy Runcible was – the drug deals, the squalid sexual favours, all of them convinced Neil without interesting him very much. The descent into prostitution happened all the time, too. But it was the characters who Neil didn't find convincing. They didn't seem to have a real background, like the teenagers he took into custody. And they didn't speak like them. Most of the time they were awkward, more inarticulate than the kids Neil knew. Every now and then, however, one would come up with some sharp line or witty insight which reminded him of Melanie's show-off university friends.

Melanie. He wondered what she'd made of the play. At least, what she'd made of the first half, which was all she'd seen of it. He wondered when she'd get round to calling him, giving him the news about her relationship with Peter Whiteside. Or would she just turn up for their date on Saturday as though nothing was going on?

"What do you think of Lynda Crabbe, then?" Dylan asked in the interval.

"I'd rather have seen Anna Derbyshire with her kit off," Neil confessed.

"Dream on, son. But Lynda, she's fairly fit, isn't she? You know, when I interviewed her last night, she was definitely interested."

"A woman interested, yet you didn't proposition her that very instant?"

"She's a murder suspect, isn't she?"

"Not a very serious one," Neil pointed out.

"I thought I might have another word with her backstage."

Neil laughed. "She might not be so interested now that she's the star."

"You think not?" Dylan said, thoughtfully.

"I don't know," Neil said, his mind returning to Melanie. Should he ring her? "Go and see her," he told Dylan. "She can only turn you down."

"I might, at that. What do you think of the play, then?"

"I can understand why so many people are leaving," Neil said, as the foyer doors swung open and shut with more departing theatre-goers.

"I think it's pretty good myself. Life-like, know what I mean? Better than most of the tame stuff they put on the goggle box." But Neil wasn't listening.

Melanie had just walked in through the foyer doors.

"Mrs Crane, I'm Detective Inspector Greasby. This is Constable Clare Coppola."

"Will you please tell me why you're holding my daughter?" Samantha Crane was in her mid-forties, a bony woman with steely blue eyes and hair in a tight chignon. She looked like a senior social worker or a headteacher.

"We'll get to that," Greasby said. "But, as it stands, your daughter hasn't been charged with anything. We need some more information."

"The man from the local paper said that this was all to do with Mark Murray being murdered…"

"Yes," Clare told her. "That's right."

"Have you caught the killer yet?" Clare and Greasby glanced at each other. They'd assumed that the *Post* had told Mrs Crane what Tamara had confessed to, but it sounded like Dan Rossiter had been more devious than that.

"We haven't made any arrests," Greasby said. "Can you tell us what your daughter's relationship with Murray was?"

"Which daughter?"

"Let's start with Gill."

Mrs Crane took a couple of breaths, her eyes darting between Clare and Greasby, as if deciding how much to tell them.

"What do you know about Gill?" she asked.

"We know that she's missing," Clare said, quietly.

"Has been for nearly two years. Tamara misses her terribly. They were very close."

"Do you know where she is?" Greasby asked.

"No. I've been to the police, the Missing Persons Helpline, even put an ad in *The Big Issue*, thinking that she might have gone to London, tried her luck there as an actress. But … nothing." Clare had been trying to track down Gill herself. Social Security had nothing on her. Neither had the Inland Revenue. But she could have changed her name, left the country, got married. Record systems were imperfect. And people disappeared all the time.

"Tamara believes that she's dead," Greasby put to Mrs Crane.

"I know. In some ways, that's easier than trying to hold out hope. Is that what this is all about? Gillian?"

"We want to know about her relationship with Mark Murray." Samantha Crane lit a cigarette, sucking a centimetre from it with one drag.

"There's not a lot to tell," she said. "Gill came here three years ago and worked as a waitress to support herself while she did a drama course. Met Mark. She didn't like him at first, she said, but that only made him more determined. After three months, she started going out with him. By spring, he was virtually living with her. She twice brought him to stay with us in Norwich.

"Things got rocky, though, by the summer. Gill told us nothing until Christmas, when she didn't bring him home with her. It seemed that, many nights when he said he was staying at his mother's, he was actually with other women. Gill only found out because somebody on her course told her. She'd confronted him and he admitted it."

"So that was the end of the relationship?" Clare asked.

"Oh no. By Easter, they were back together again. It was inevitable, Gill said. This time it was going to be different. He'd sown his wild oats, Gill reckoned, and she was more in love than ever. They were talking about getting married. He came to visit us one more time. And then…" She stared wistfully out of the window.

"What happened?" Greasby demanded.

"He got a part in that ghastly soap opera. Then he was off to London. He must have dumped Gill around the same time, but she never told us. She just stopped phoning. From then on, Gill was never in when I called. Later, when I wrote to her, my letters were returned: *addressee unknown* written on them. By the time I got in touch with the police, she was long gone. There wasn't much they could do. *She's a grown woman* they said. But she wasn't. She was my little girl."

Clare noted that *was*. It seemed that both Tamara and Samantha Crane thought that Gill was dead.

"If only I'd gone to her sooner. I might have stopped…" A single tear trailed down her cheek. Clare offered her a tissue. Samantha Crane dried her eyes then blew her nose.

"It's been nearly two years now. Two Christmases.

Two anniversaries of her father's death. She's not been in touch. That can only mean one thing. My eldest daughter's dead. And it's Mark Murray's fault!"

10

"What are you doing here?" Neil asked Melanie, trying to act normal.

"I thought I'd join you for the second half of the play. But you seem to have company."

"Don't worry. There's loads of spare seats."

"That's not what I meant, really," she said, glancing at Dylan.

"Excuse me," the DS said, tactfully. "Need a word with the stage manager."

"What is it?" Neil asked, once he was out of earshot. Melanie wasn't dressed for the theatre. She was still wearing the jeans and sweater she'd had on earlier, when he'd seen her with Whiteside.

"I'm sorry I snapped at you on the phone," she said.

"It's all right," Neil replied. He would, he realized, do or say whatever was needed to keep her.

"The thing is, I was at this play last night."

"Oh."

"I'm meant to be reviewing it for the university newspaper."

"Right," Neil said.

"Then I saw you in the interval and I thought…"

"You thought what?"

"This is going to sound silly but, since I moved out, you've been getting all possessive, wanting to know where I've been, who I've seen. So I thought, that … well, that you were spying on me."

"You're kidding!" Neil blushed. She was right about the possessiveness, the jealousy. But she was wrong about last night.

Mel shook her head, shamefaced. "Thing is, I was with this guy, Pete. He was reviewing it too. But it might have looked like a date. So, when I saw you, I freaked… I told him I felt ill and walked out."

"But it wasn't a date…?" Neil asked, trying to put an amused note in his voice.

"No, I mean. He might be interested, but…"

"I wouldn't blame anyone for being interested in you." So Clare was right! The guy was fantasizing, thinking that he was Mel's boyfriend.

"Anyway, I felt a bit silly when I read about Mark Murray being murdered. Then, when you rang asking if I wanted to come tonight, I figured you were getting at me somehow. Which, I realize, was also silly. So here I am. I thought I'd see the second half, then at least I'd be able to review it."

"Great," Neil said, kissing her lightly on the cheek. "Only thing is, I need to hang around afterwards."

"And I'll need to go home and write my review," Melanie said. She must have seen the disappointment in Neil's face, because she added: "Then why don't you come and join me when you're through?"

"Great," he said, as the bell went for the end of the interval and he felt a huge weight lifting from him. He was even looking forward to the second half. Maybe the play wasn't so bad after all.

To charge or not to charge? Clare was glad that it wasn't her decision. Tamara Crane had admitted to murder. She had given them motive and means, but no actual proof. Tamara had not been identified as being at the hotel or the radio station. If the police were lucky, they would find somebody who remembered her buying a bronze statuette on Monday. But even that would not be proof in itself. They could send divers into the part of the Trent where Tamara claimed to have slung the murder weapon. But she'd been vague about the location. There was no guarantee that they'd find the statuette, or that there would be traces of Mark Murray's blood on the thing if they did.

Yet Tamara had confessed. Her confession was on

tape. Her mother, having heard what Tamara claimed to have done, was arranging a solicitor. The solicitor, when he or she arrived, would doubtless advise Tamara not to tell the police any more than she had told them already. So the police had little to lose by holding back.

Ian Jagger arrived at five past nine. Mrs Crane had evidently decided to hire the best.

"I read about your engagement in today's paper," Clare told him. "Do pass on my congratulations to Charlene."

"Thank you," Jagger said. "I'm sorry. You are..." Vaguely humiliated, she told him her name. "Of course," Jagger said, his smile suddenly sympathetic. "You were very close to the late Inspector Grace, I believe. Please accept my condolences." Clare nodded. She was predisposed to dislike Jagger, but his words seemed genuine enough. The DI returned and Jagger greeted him.

"Ah, John, how are you?"

"Not bad, Ian. You?" Greasby shook the solicitor's hand.

"In my prime, old lad, in my prime."

"Wedding plans, I hear. Set a date?"

"March, we thought. First day of spring."

"Very appropriate. Congratulations."

Jagger thanked him. "Charged my girl yet?"

"Thought we'd wait for you. Make sure she still wants to confess afterwards."

"Are you suggesting that I put words into my clients' mouths, Detective Inspector?" Jagger asked, with a wry grin. Both men laughed. They knew each other socially, Clare could tell. Where? The Rotary Club, somewhere like that. Paul had been planning to join before he died. *You need every prop you can find to help you climb the greasy pole* he'd said. Though he drew the line at joining the free-masons. *Counts against you with some people these days.* Ben Shipman suspected Jagger of being the front man for a racist group. But how could that be if he was marrying a black woman? Unless Charlene was unknowingly being used as cover. No. Clare knew Charlene a little. She was far too smart to be taken in.

"You'd better take me to her, then," Jagger said, and Greasby led him away.

"That's you for the day," the DI told Clare when he returned. "There won't be anything doing until tomorrow morning now."

"I'll be in at eight," Clare said. That would give her time for a swim first.

"All right. Though I should warn you, if this stands up and we've got a result, you'll be back in uniform by the afternoon."

Clare left. That was all she needed: back on the beat with her dodgy ankle and working from eight in the morning until ten in the evening two days' running. She sincerely hoped that Tamara Crane was making it up, for whatever reason. Because if she was, it meant that Clare could stay on the case.

Neil, ecstatic that Melanie was with him, found it hard to concentrate on the second half. Mel would be off to write her review, so at least there was no need to discuss it with her afterwards. She would doubtless have some highfaluting analysis of how the play probed the British class structure or explored outlawed forms of sexuality. When she spouted that kind of stuff, Neil stopped listening. The play's ending seemed pretty weak to him: everyone ended up exactly as they'd started, concealing their wounds, pretending that nothing had happened.

Melanie gave him a quick kiss, then hurried away. After the curtain call, Neil and Dylan headed backstage. Paul Santiago was waiting for them.

"You had something to tell us," Dylan said. The director waited until none of the actors were in earshot. "You noticed that Anna Derbyshire wasn't here today?"

"Could hardly miss it," Neil commented, ruefully.

"She's quit," Santiago told them. "Left a scrawled note saying that she's ill. Gone back to Trudy in London."

"And that's what you wanted to tell us?" Dylan asked.

"It's unheard of, losing your two main actors that

way. We've got a week in Leeds and another in Newcastle to do. We'll be lucky to get any audience at all."

"We sympathize," Neil said. "But…"

"It's not your problem, I know. The point is, I spoke to Anna this morning. She seemed in shock about Mark, but she didn't say anything about leaving. And then the note … it was her handwriting, but very scrawled. Anna and I go back a long way – she'd have phoned me, at the very least."

"You think there's something suspicious about her going?"

"In a word, yes. I mean, it's career suicide, for a start. If she doesn't produce a doctor's certificate, she'll never work for the Royal Court again."

"We'll see what we can find out," Neil told him.

"Something doesn't smell right," Dylan said, when they were alone.

"What do you think made her leave?" Neil asked. "Guilt?"

"Or fear," Dylan suggested.

"In which case, you have to ask *who benefits*? The only people I can think of are the understudies. Neither of them has an alibi for Murray's murder." Chris winked.

"Looks like I'll have to talk to Lynda Crabbe again."

"You do that," Neil said, anxious now to get to Melanie's.

"See you in the morning, all right?" As Dylan was leaving, Steve Garrett came by, talking to Paul Santiago. He looked pleased as punch.

"What're you doing here?" Neil asked Steve.

"This is our new understudy," Santiago explained. "Are we done?"

"For now, yes," Neil said, nodding at Steve. So Garrett had a motive for killing Mark Murray, too. It had led to his first decent acting job. Even if he never had to perform, Steve could say that he had worked for the Royal Court. That had to be worth a lot.

There were far too many suspects in this case, Neil thought, as he drove up the hill to Melanie's. He hadn't the least idea which one of them had done it.

11

"Well?" Dan Rossiter said at seven forty-five, as Clare came in through the door. "There's less than an hour to my deadline. We had a deal."

"I'm just waiting for her solicitor," Greasby informed him. "He spent an hour with her last night. Then, presuming she hasn't changed her story overnight, we'll be charging her with murder."

"Y-E-S!" Rossiter got out a mobile phone and called his newsroom.

"Go with headline one. Leave para two blank. I'll call in the copy asap."

Jagger arrived. He wasn't alone. His wife-to-be, Charlene Harris, wore a mid-length, slim cut, matt-black leather jacket, a sharp contrast to her fiancé's suit.

"Ms Harris would like five minutes with our client before you charge her," Ian Jagger told DI Greasby. "Would that be all right?"

"Of course."

"I'm on a tight deadline here," Dan Rossiter reminded them.

"I hope that this case is not being prosecuted at the convenience of the press," Jagger remarked, dryly.

"Of course not. Clare, take Ms Harris through, would you?"

"Sir." She led the solicitor down to the cells, not sure how to treat her. Were they friends, acquaintances or professionals at odds with each other?

"Are you going to show us your ring, then?" she asked, when they were alone. Charlene smiled and held up the elegant, diamond-studded, silver ring.

"Fantastic," she said. "Congratulations."

"Thanks," Charlene said, brusquely. "Tell me, have you met this Tamara Crane?"

"I sat in on her interviews, yes."

"How did you find her?"

Clare thought for a moment. "Suspicious," she said. "Normally, when people confess, it all comes spilling out, full of guilt and unwittingly incriminating detail. But all Tamara seems to care about is badmouthing Mark Murray. The fact of having killed someone doesn't seem to have touched her at all."

"Thanks," Charlene said. "It's funny, 'suspicious' is the word Ian used. That's why he wants me to have a go. Can't see it working myself." She paused. "Listen, I was really sorry about Paul..."

"I got your card," Clare said. "Thanks."

"It wasn't much."

"Not many people sent anything," Clare said. "I was only the *girlfriend*."

"You want to go for a drink sometime? Catch up?"

"I'd like that," Clare told her. They exchanged phone numbers. Charlene gave Clare two: one for her flat, one for Ian Jagger's place. That's a turn-up, Clare thought, as she returned to the incident room, me and Charlene becoming friendly. When Ruth was going out with Ben, it would have been impossible. But now, why not?

Ian Jagger had brought in the morning papers. Mark Murray's death led all of the tabloids and was front page news in the broadsheets too. "SOAP STAR SLAIN IN HOTEL ROOM" was how the *Sun* put it. "Police baffled by actor's murder" said its sister paper, *The Times*. The *Mirror* had an exclusive. "JEALOUS LOVER COULD HAVE KILLED MARK! *He had it coming, says soap star's ex*."

"Which 'ex' is that?" Greasby asked, as Clare read the story. She turned to an inside page. What if the *Mirror* had tracked down Gill Crane, who her sister believed to be dead?

"It's somebody called Janine Taylor," Jagger informed them.

That was all right, then. Dylan had interviewed Janine, found little of use. Clare glanced at the story: the girl had no real information, just speculation based on the number of times Mark Murray had cheated on her. Clare could have told the paper more about Mark Murray's character than Janine had.

Tamara Crane greeted Charlene confidently. A night in a police cell didn't seem to have daunted her.

"Do you know what you'll get?" Charlene asked, after explaining who she was. "There's no chance of having the charge reduced to manslaughter. You might have a sob story to tell, but you're still going to get twelve to fifteen years for premeditated murder. With good behaviour, you'll serve ten. That's a long time."

"Then I'll be twenty-seven when I come out," Tamara told her. "Most of my life ahead of me. Unlike Gill."

"Why are you so sure that your sister's dead?" Charlene asked.

"She would have been in touch if she wasn't."

"Does your mother feel the same?"

"My mother's got nothing to do with this," Tamara snapped.

"I see." Something clicked. Mother and daughter in league together? Maybe that was the suspicious something that both Ian and Clare had seen: Tamara was covering up her mother's role in Mark Murray's murder.

"Why wait 'til now?" Charlene asked. "It's been two years since…"

Tamara shrugged sullenly. "Things … fester in you. And I needed an opportunity. I needed to know where Mark was. When he was on the telly, there were people around him all the time. You couldn't get close."

"You tried?"

"Once or twice, yeah."

Charlene had a thought. "Tell me," she said, "did you ever try and sell Gill's story to the papers?"

Tamara looked shifty as she replied. "I rang one of them once, yeah."

"But they didn't bite?"

"They said that without Gill, or proof that she was dead, there was no story."

"I see," Charlene said, standing up. "They're going to charge you now, Tamara. Before they do, I ought to warn you about something."

"What?" the girl asked, edgy now, thinking that Charlene knew something she didn't.

"The police in this city have a policy about people wasting police time, for whatever reason. You wouldn't believe how many people make false allegations, false confessions, too. The policy is that, once someone wastes over a hundred police hours, they always prosecute. By my calculations, you've used up only twenty or thirty hours so far. But, today, they'll be diverting loads of officers to find evidence to back up your confession. They'll reach a hundred by lunchtime, easy. And, if you didn't do it, not only are you wasting police time, but you're stopping the police from looking for the real murderer. Magistrates take a very dim view of that kind of thing."

"What are you saying?"

"I'm saying that, even if you withdraw your confession later on and produce an airtight alibi, you might well end up doing three months to a year in prison."

Tamara tried to look affronted, but it was an act: "Why would I make a false confession?"

"To destroy Mark Murray's reputation, to get revenge for your sister."

"You're sick," Tamara said.

"Am I?" Charlene left the cell and rejoined Ian Jagger and the others.

"She still wants to confess."

"All right," DI Greasby said, as the reporter reached for his mobile phone. "Let's charge her."

12

"Wake up, loverboy."

"What time is it?" Chris Dylan asked, as he rolled over in a large double bed. The first thing he smelt was the big bunch of flowers perched on the dresser. Lynda had moved into Anna Derbyshire's room as soon as she took over her role.

"Just gone eight," she called from the bathroom.

Chris had to be at work in an hour. He should show up early while they were involved in a murder case. He dressed without showering.

"Will I see you tonight?" Lynda asked.

"Can't," he said. "It's my weekend to have the kids."

"You've got kids?"

"Two."

"So what are you, divorced, separated or merely pretending to be single?"

"Whichever makes you most comfortable," Dylan quipped, and she laughed.

"So this is it, then," Lynda said, coming out of the bathroom wearing only a towel. "Thanks for last night."

"Thank you." He kissed her on the forehead. Lynda was a good foot shorter than him and leaning down strained his back.

"Let's hope no one else got killed last night," she said. "Though at least I'd have the ideal alibi." Chris gave a hollow laugh. He'd come to see Lynda to find out if she knew anything about Anna Derbyshire's departure. She'd convinced him that she didn't, then poured him a drink, insisting that she needed someone to celebrate her big break with. They had done a lot of celebrating.

"Are you sure I can't order breakfast for you?" Lynda asked now.

"I'll get something at the station." He got out quickly. This was the first time he'd been with an actress, and a star, at that, if only an accidental one. Chris felt exhilarated. He could get his ex-wife to have the kids this weekend, he supposed. Plead pressure of work. With a murder on, the overtime was bound to be available. Then he could have two more nights with Lynda before she moved on. It would be the perfect relationship: short AND intense. No time to get bored with one another. No guilt at the end.

"Uh, sorry." He'd bumped into Jeremy Eaton, the understudy who had taken Mark Murray's part.

"Were you after me?" the actor asked.

"No, but…" Dylan didn't know what to say. Should he pretend to be on duty, protect Lynda's honour? "You were very good last night," he mumbled.

"Thanks." The actor backed into his small room. The hotel wouldn't have been able to give him Murray's suite. It was still sealed off as a scene-of-crime.

Dylan hurried to the station. He grabbed a sausage sandwich in the canteen, then went up to the incident room. DI Greasby was already there, as was Clare Coppola.

"Chris, good – you're early. I want you to drop whatever you're doing and check some antiques shops with Clare."

"Anything you say, boss. Before we go, I rechecked Lynda Crabbe's alibi. No witnesses at the cinema yet, but she seems solid to me."

"We've charged someone, Chris. Tamara Crane, sister of one of Murray's ex-girlfriends. Revenge killing, it seems. Clare'll bring you up to speed. We need to gather as much evidence as we can before lunchtime. I'm doing a press conference at twelve and I'd like a few witnesses to place this girl before her picture's in the evening paper. I did try calling you at home to get you in early, but you didn't return my message. Out last night, were you?"

Chris grinned. "You could have page me."

"It wasn't all that urgent," Greasby said, dismissing him.

"Where are we going?" Chris asked Clare, after she'd filled him in on Tamara Crane's confession.

"Antiques shops on the Derby Road, but they won't be open yet. The boss also wants us to check out Gill Crane, the accuser's sister, see if we can find some old friends who might know what happened to her."

"I thought you said that she'd topped herself?"

"That's what Tamara thinks. Doesn't mean it's true. I've got one address from her mum – a woman in Mapperley who Gill used to lodge with. I just phoned. We can catch her in if we go now."

"Let's do it then."

Meg Johnson was a twenty-two-year-old credit controller with a one-year-old kid, who she was about to deposit in a nursery for the day.

"I've got ten minutes," she told Chris and Clare.

"We don't need that long," Chris told her. "It's about Gill Crane. I believe you were a friend of hers."

"I was, yes." She didn't look at the two detectives

but continued spooning baby food into the child's mouth.

"When did you last see her?" Clare asked.

"I don't remember. A year or two ago. Actually, it's more like two, because she didn't come to my wedding. I would've invited her, if I'd known where she was. I remember trying to track her down. Her mum said that there'd been some kind of family row, they didn't have an address."

"Family row?" Clare repeated. "Do you know what it was about?"

"No. It was a long time ago. I may have got it wrong."

"Did you know Mark Murray?" Chris asked.

"We were on the same course, yes. Is this about his death?"

"It's connected," Chris told her.

"Gill was besotted with him. But it turned out badly."

"Do you know how it ended?" Clare.

"He went to London."

"You kept in touch with Gill after that?" Clare again.

"Yes, until she … disappeared."

"And you've no idea where she is now?" Chris.

"No," Meg Johnson shook her head vigorously. "None at all."

"Thanks for your time," Chris said, handing her a card. "If you think of anything which might help us to track Gill down, please call us on this number."

"What did you think?" he asked Clare once they were in the car.

"She knew more than she was saying," Clare speculated.

"Maybe she was another one of Mark Murray's conquests and that's why they fell out. Did that occur to you?"

"Yes, you can never discount that possibility with Mark. Maybe that's all it was."

Chris remembered something.

"Didn't you grow up with Murray?"

"Sort of. Our mums are friends."

"Did you and he ever?"

"No!" Clare looked affronted.

"I'd be surprised if he hadn't tried, that was all," Chris said, apologetically.

"I didn't say he hadn't tried," Clare told him, her voice a little edgy.

"Not your type?"

Clare frowned. "More yours, I'd say." Chris didn't know how to react to that, but he wasn't going to let Clare get away with it.

"What do you mean?" he asked.

Clare smiled cryptically. "Do I have to spell it out?"

"Yeah," Chris said, feeling confident. "Why not? Teach me something."

"All right." Clare thought for a moment. "Some women will go for a casual thing with a good-looking bloke because all they want is a bit of fun."

"Sounds right." Like Lynda. Or Clare's friend, Ruth.

"Which is fine, as far as it goes. But some are more desperate. They might go for someone like Mark – or you – because they mislead themselves into thinking casual could become serious. More fool them, you might say." Chris could think of at least a dozen women who fitted into that category. More trouble than they were worth, in the long run, but not easy to spot. Clare went on. "Most women, most of the time, only want something that looks like it might become serious from the start. They're not going to go out with someone who tries it on with anything that has two legs, two tits and a heartbeat." Chris gave an empty chuckle. Clare wasn't usually crude. Maybe she thought that it was the only way to get through to him. He waited, but she seemed to have finished.

"So that's why you didn't go out with Mark?" he said.

"Sort of."

"And why you wouldn't go out with me?"

"I don't recall you asking," Clare said, diplomatically, looking away. Had he? Chris recalled trying it on with her, but not the specifics.

"If I had…" he said, pausing to allow a question to form.

"I'm not interested in anybody in the foreseeable future," Clare turned round and looked at him directly, so that he was forced, for a moment, to take his eyes off the road. "And even if I were, you're not my type. No offence meant."

"None taken," Dylan told her, telling himself that he wasn't bothered. He didn't fancy Clare half as much since she'd put on weight and he'd rather date an actress than a policewoman any day.

13

Sometimes, Jo went home for lunch. Mum and Dad were at work, so she wasn't really meant to, but it was nice to take a couple of mates back for a giggle. They'd play tapes, eat their packed lunches, pretend to be models or film stars. A couple of times, she and her mate Sandra had brought boys back. But it had nearly got out of hand. They'd wanted to get the girls in separate rooms, take liberties.

Today she'd gone home alone. Mark Murray's death had depressed her. She hated it when kids at school teased her about him. They had Jo down as this great fantasist when, actually, she hadn't told them half the story, how he'd talked to her, then kissed her goodbye. She'd remembered every word of the conversation, written it down so that she would never forget it. She had described every moment of the kiss, too. Not that she was likely to forget that.

At home, Jo checked Teletext to see if there was any news about Mark's murder. All it said was that the police were giving a press conference at midday. The time was past that now, but no new news appeared. Jo tried to write a poem about Mark. There was an English teacher who she showed her poems to sometimes, who encouraged her. But the words all came out wrong and, if anyone other than the teacher saw it, they would laugh at her.

She went back to school early so that she could stop at the newsagents to buy the evening paper. There was one of those boards outside the shop which gave the main headline. When Jo saw what it said, she began to run.

"MURRAY MURDERER ARRESTED!"

Breathlessly, she handed over her money and took a paper from the top of the pile. There was a colour photo of an attractive teenage girl: not, at first glance, very different from Jo herself. Jo took in the picture first, then read the sensational headline: "MARK MURRAY DROVE MY SISTER TO SUICIDE! POST EXCLUSIVE. NAKED SEVENTEEN YEAR OLD SLAUGHTERED SOAP STAR!"

Jo couldn't believe it. Surely the murder was the

result of a robbery which went wrong? But she pored over the paper as she went back to school, walking slowly, not caring if she were late. It was such a sordid tale: Mark Murray getting famous and abandoning an ex-girlfriend who then killed herself. It didn't sound like the Mark that she'd met. But it was in the paper, so it must be true.

Only it wasn't true! There, buried in the continuation of the story on page three was a bare-faced lie! How did this girl have the nerve? And if she'd lied about this, what else had she lied about?

"Jo? What's wrong?" It was Natalie Loscoe, also late back. She'd probably been meeting up with her boyfriend, Curt Wilder.

"Have you seen the paper?"

"No."

"Look at this," Jo said. "It's all lies, every word of it!"

Clare and Chris got back to the station at one. They'd covered every antiques shop on the Derby Road, and then some. Nobody remembered selling a bronze figurine to a woman resembling the photograph they had of Tamara Crane, not on Monday, or any other recent day of the week. They told Greasby this.

"Seen Dan Rossiter's story?" the DI asked, passing over the *Evening Post*, which had a sleazy headline. The paper's photo of Tamara Crane made her look like a Page Three girl about to take her kit off. Clare made a dismissive comment.

"There's a discrepancy with what she told us," Greasby pointed out. "Flick to the end." Clare and Chris read the bit he pointed out. Clare finished it first.

"It says that she showed him the way to the restaurant. That's not what she told us."

"Correct," Greasby said.

"And if she was lying about that," Clare said, "then maybe the whole confession…"

"Precisely." Greasby.

"Have you asked her about it?" Dylan asked the DI.

"No. She'd probably say that the *Post* put the words in her mouth."

"I recall her hesitating when we asked her about that," Clare pointed out.

"Me too," Greasby said. "I've replayed the tape. Also, I've asked Dan Rossiter to bring in his original tape of Tamara Crane's interview with the *Post*. We want to know exactly what she said before we tackle her again."

"Have you told the Detective Superintendent?" Dylan asked. Greasby rolled his eyes as if to say *you must be joking*. "She'll love it, won't she – only an hour since she gave a press conference announcing that we've caught the murderer, we take it all back, say that she's just a silly kid who made the whole thing up. I take it that you didn't find anything to confirm her story?"

"Nothing at all," Clare said. "But there is one good thing. Presuming that Tamara did make her confession up, then the real murderer's out there feeling remarkably safe at the moment. Maybe whoever did it will get overconfident, give themselves away."

"Oh, sure," Dylan said, in his most cynical voice. "If they don't kill again."

14

Neil caught the 11.33 to St Pancras, which got him into London ten minutes later than advertised, at 13.41. He hadn't informed Trudy Runcible or Anna Derbyshire that he was coming to see them. He didn't want the actress or the writer aware that the police were suspicious about the way Derbyshire had left the touring production of *Selling England*.

Trudy Runcible was "workshopping" her next play, *Screwed*, at the Royal Court Upstairs. Neil took a taxi to her house in Willesden, then wished that he'd used the tube. When they turned on to Fleetwood Road, Neil was surprised by the leafiness of the street, and by the houses, which were big, Edwardian semis with three or four bedrooms, garages at the side and tidy gardens at the back. Family homes. Not the kind of area where you'd expect a hip, twenty-something playwright to live.

Neil got the taxi to wait in case Anna Derbyshire wasn't home. She wasn't. So much for her illness. The driver took him to Willesden Green tube station. The Jubilee line took Neil to the West End in fifteen minutes. Getting admission to the rehearsal took longer. First he had to knock on a door for ages, then the jobsworth who answered didn't want to disturb the very important director and actors who were working inside. Neil's warrant card didn't impress him.

"This says Nottingham. You're in London now, mate. I'm paid to keep people like you out. Important creative work going on in there."

"What does it mean," Neil asked, " 'work-shopping' a play?"

"Trudy making it up with the actors as she goes along," said a new voice from inside.

"What was that?" Neil looked over the security guy's shoulders. The actor who'd spoken was coming down the stairs from the workshop.

"Let me through will you? I'm dying for a smoke."

"Is Trudy up there?" Neil asked.

"Yeah. We're on a break." Neil hurried up the stairs before the security guy could think of another reason to stop him. Trudy Runcible was in the corridor, adjusting her crumpled overalls as she walked. She looked more like a painter and decorator than a playwright.

"Remember me?" Neil said. It took her a moment. "Nottingham, yes. What are you doing here?"

"It's about Anna." It wasn't just about Anna, actually. He was also intending to check Trudy's alibi for the night of Mark Murray's death. Though why Trudy would want to kill Murray, Neil didn't know.

"What about Anna? Is she ill?"

"I presume so," Neil said.

"You *presume*? What are you going on about?"

"She walked out of the tour claiming illness."

"Anna walked out?" The surprise on Trudy's face seemed genuine. "Anna wouldn't desert a play unless she was strapped to a hospital bed. What *are* you going on about?"

"Perhaps we'd better sit down," Neil said. "Somewhere private."

"Paul Santiago got a note from Anna," Neil explained, when they'd found a small office. "It said that she had to leave in a hurry 'for health reasons'." Now Trudy looked more than concerned. "It must have been very sudden, then. She would have told me. We talked nearly every night before she went to bed."

"Last night?"

"I was at a party."

Neil nodded impatiently. "So you've no idea where she is?"

"No. You're getting me worried. At home, I guess."

"There's no one in. I've just been there."

"You'd better let me get to a phone," Trudy said. "I want to sort out what's going on."

Neil watched as she went to a payphone, dialled her home number, then pressed the code which allowed her to access messages from her answering machine. When Trudy returned, her perplexed expression had changed to one of deep anxiety.

"Nothing from Anna."

"Is there anywhere … anyone who she would have gone to see? Family? Old friends?"

"I don't think so," Trudy said. "Not without telling me. Let me call our doctor, see if she's been in touch with her. Would you give me some privacy?" Neil waited in the corridor while she made a call, which didn't last long. When Trudy returned, her voice began to rise. "Where the hell is she? You've got to do something. This isn't like Anna at all. You've got to find out where she is as soon as possible. Something must have happened to her!"

Tamara Crane's *Evening Post* interview was on tape. Dan Rossiter was helping Clare and DI Greasby to find the relevant section.

"I think this is it," Rossiter told Clare, and turned up the volume. She and Greasby listened to the interview recorded the day before. Rossiter spoke first.

"You've been in Nottingham since Monday, so why wait until Wednesday to kill him?"

"I had to get Mark on his own," Tamara replied. "I hung around near the Theatre Royal and waited. I followed him."

"It was you on Tuesday night, was it? The one who showed him the way to a restaurant?"

"Who told you about that?" Tamara asked. "The police?"

"No, the doorman at the Theatre Royal. You meant to attack Mark then, but he was meeting a woman in the restaurant, so you didn't get your chance."

"No."

"So the next day you waited for him outside Radio Trent?"

"Yes."

Rossiter was doing too much of the talking, Clare thought, not giving Tamara room to add telling details. That *no* was ambiguous. It could mean *no, I didn't get a chance* or it could mean *no, I wasn't there*. But Rossiter had rushed on. He'd never make a detective.

"Where he proposed that you go back to his hotel room?"

"Something like that, yes." Tamara was being evasive. There was more to this story than she was letting on, Clare thought. She wanted to show Mark in as bad a light as possible. Was she making it all up?

"Mark didn't recognize you from when he was going out with your sister?"

"I've changed a lot since I was fifteen."

DI Greasby stopped the tape. Clare spoke to Rossiter.

"You gave her the information about walking Murray to the restaurant. She didn't supply any details."

"The doorman was the only person I spoke to about it. He said that a girl waiting outside told Murray how to find the place and they walked off together."

"You didn't ask Tamara what they talked about?"

"I assumed she got his autograph and left."

"You see," Greasby said, "in our interview, Tamara told us that it wasn't her on Tuesday night." Rossiter saw at once what he was getting at. "If she was lying about that, she could be lying about everything else."

"Precisely," Greasby said. "But she didn't exactly lie."

"She didn't correct me, either," Rossiter said.

"It's possible that she was tired at that point of the interview," Clare said. "Not listening properly.

After all, the other parts of our interview fit perfectly."

"True," Greasby said.

"I think we should put out a radio appeal to the other girls who were waiting outside Radio Trent," Clare suggested. "See if we can find a witness to confirm that Tamara met Mark there."

"Can't hurt," Greasby said. "I'll get the press office to give them a ring. Then we'd better call Ian Jagger, arrange to reinterview Tamara Crane. I want you to bring in the woman from the restaurant again, see if she recognizes Tamara."

Trudy Runcible returned to Nottingham with Neil on the 1600 train, the two of them packed tightly together in a twin seat. Frequently, she burst into tears.

"This is probably a simple misunderstanding," he tried to tell her. "Maybe she'll be back in the play tonight." But he didn't believe it. Trudy had spoken to Paul Santiago earlier. He'd said that Anna's note had been clear. And Paul knew her well. There was no doubt of the handwriting being hers. Maybe this was a lovers' tiff, Neil thought. Anna was walking out on Trudy and the play. One thing was for sure. The playwright hadn't killed Mark Murray. He'd spoken to the cast of her new play and they'd each confirmed that she was in London working with them when she said she was.

Neil had left his car at the railway station, so dropped Trudy at the Theatre Royal then went over to the police station. He should be through for the day now, but wasn't surprised to find Dylan, Greasby and Clare still in the incident room. Greasby told him about the discrepancy between Tamara Crane's police statement and her *Evening Post* interview.

"She'll probably argue that the reporter put words in her mouth, and she let him believe it because she thought it made a better story."

"So now you think that the whole thing's lies?" Neil asked.

"She's standing by the rest of it," Greasby said. "We're trying to find more holes in her confession."

"And I'm trying to find Anna Derbyshire."

"I checked the hotel," Dylan told him. "Derbyshire was last seen there at four yesterday afternoon."

"We need a break," Greasby said. "We're not getting anywhere. The theatre people leave Nottingham on Sunday morning. We'd better reinterview all of them tomorrow. I'll make sure that they're all in the hotel. Tonight, I want everyone to take a break. We'll reconvene at nine in the morning. Be prepared to work a twelve hour day. All right?"

No one argued, though Dylan muttered something about childcare. Neil, however, was angry. He was meant to be taking Melanie out for a meal. It was her twentieth birthday tomorrow. How would he make it up to her?

Rather than go straight home, he drove to Wellington Square and rang Mel's doorbell. There was no reply. He had her spare key with him, so let himself in. After the night before, he had no qualms about going in and waiting for her. He'd been in a needless, paranoid panic about Peter Whiteside.

He went through to the bedroom, took off his shoes, then lay down on the bed. He didn't know why he was so exhausted – most of his day had been taken up by train journeys. But he was tired, and less than a minute passed before he was fast asleep.

Penelope Palmer now said that Tamara Crane definitely wasn't the girl she'd seen outside the restaurant with Mark.

"The girl he came with was younger than her. I was a little shocked. The woman he was meeting was the same age as him, after all! Of course, you read about such things…"

"You're certain?" Clare asked.

"Yes. It was dark out, but there was plenty of light from the restaurant. That's not her."

Tamara was an attention seeker, Clare decided, not a murderer.

Jagger spent half an hour with his client, then agreed to a second interview, which Clare, Dylan and Greasby attended.

"You told the Evening Post reporter that you walked with Mark to Stokely's restaurant," Greasby reminded Tamara. "Why didn't you tell us that?"

"Because it wasn't true," Tamara said. "I didn't tell the reporter I walked to any restaurant. He may have asked something about it, I don't recall what I said. I was outside the Theatre Royal on Tuesday, watching. But I didn't see Mark leave that night. He got away by a back door." Tamara hadn't been caught out in a lie, Clare decided, not quite.

"All right," Greasby said. "Now, I want to go over how you got into Mark's room. Yesterday, you said – or should I say *implied* that Mark recognized you, invited you back to his room and you went on ahead. Is that how it happened?" Tamara looked at Jagger, who nodded.

"No," she said. "Mark didn't recognize me. I've changed a lot since he saw me last and, anyway, I only met him twice when he was going out with my sister."

"So how did you introduce yourself?"

"I told him that he knew my brother, Warren."

"Is there a Warren?"

"Not as far as I know, but it gave me a start over the girls and explained why he might find me familiar looking. He said do you want to catch up back at the hotel, told me his room number."

"And gave you the key?"

"No. He'd left the door open."

This was the first time *that* detail had emerged. Who left their hotel door unlocked? Though, in Mark's case, Clare could almost believe it. He probably made a habit of picking up girls on the street. No wonder she'd been coy about it. Clare could almost hear Mark saying: *just go on up, babe, the door's open.*

"So you went in, took all your clothes off…"

"My client has been through all of this before," Jagger butted in. "You have her confession. If there are any new facts that you wish to establish…"

"Do you still contend that you killed Mark Murray?" the DI asked.

"My client has already answered that question," Jagger said, bringing the interview to an abrupt end. So he had his doubts, too. The solicitor had a high opinion of himself. He wouldn't like being played for a fool any more than the police did.

"She didn't do it," Clare said, when solicitor and client were gone.

"If she didn't," Dylan said, gloomily, "then who did?"

15

The bedroom door opened and Neil woke instantly. Outside, it was pitch black. He must have been asleep for ages. As Melanie switched on the light, he sat up. He didn't want to scare her, but it was too late not to give her a shock. The clock on the wall said ten to ten.

"Hi."

Mel almost hit the ceiling. "Sorry," he added, as she stared at him. "I decided to wait for you and fell asleep."

"I'm not meant to be seeing you until tomorrow night," she replied, coldly.

"I know, but…"

"I've got company."

"I thought…" It was the way she said *company*. He knew, at once, what it meant.

"Mel?" A voice from the other room, a voice that Neil had only heard on the telephone before but recognized immediately: Peter Whiteside.

"This is really awkward," she said.

"He doesn't know about me?" Neil asked, his voice dull but deliberate. She shook her head. "Not exactly."

"Well, he does now," Neil said, as the bedroom door opened wider. Whiteside walked into the room, put a proprietorial arm around Melanie's waist and said "Wha…?" before seeing Neil, still sitting up on the bed.

"I think you've got some explaining to do," Neil told Mel, which was a pretty weak thing to say because the situation explained itself. All Mel said was:

"I think you'd better give me my key back." Neil reached into his pocket for it. "Could you wait in the other room?" she asked Whiteside.

"If you're sure it's OK."

"What are you going to tell him?" Neil asked Melanie once he was gone. "That I'm an ex-boyfriend who came round to return your key?"

"He knows about you," Mel said, softly. "I told him how important you'd been to me and that I was trying to break up with you but withdraw gently. I'm sorry, Neil. I didn't want to hurt you any more than… I guess it's too late now."

"When were you going to tell me?" Neil asked, bitterly.

"I dunno. Before Christmas."

"Why?" Neil asked, plaintively. "Why?"

"Pete and I have so much more in common than you and I do. He's…"

"It's the job, isn't it?" Neil interrupted. "You hate the job."

"I don't like that you spend half your time dealing with low-lifes and violence, no. But the long and short of it is – I'm not in love with you any more." There was no reply to that. Neil put on his coat and left with as much dignity as he could muster. He'd hidden her present, an expensive leather jacket from Next, beneath her bed. She'd find it one day and work out where it came from. Or not. Who cared?

Gary was on patrol with Ben Shipman. The November streets were quiet, a biting cold having come in from the north, though the two of them were warm enough in the car. Ben, often bad-tempered, seemed in a good mood tonight. Mind you, nobody had dared to tell him that his ex was engaged to marry a man he hated. Gary had no intention of bringing up the subject himself. Nor had Jan Hunt, their sergeant, though it was her who had told Gary earlier, before Ben got in.

Ben shouldn't be upset. He had a new sweetheart

to go home to. Everything between him and Julie seemed hunky-dory. Though what Ben was doing shacked up in a slum with a seventeen-year-old single mother, Gary would never work out.

On London Road, there had been construction work going on for as long as Gary had been in Nottingham, probably a hell of a lot longer. On the night shift, Gary and Ben would occasionally stop by to visit the nightwatchman, Ted Needy, check that everything was OK. But this wasn't the night shift. This was two minutes to ten on the afternoon shift and they were heading back to the station to clock off when Ted came running out into the road, waving his arms. Gary made an emergency stop.

"You need to come quick," Ted said, "before it sinks."

"Before what sinks?" Ben asked.

"Quick. C'mon. This way."

They locked the car and, torches in hand, followed Ted into the foundations of what would one day be a gymnasium aimed at the assorted journalists, income tax officers and businessmen who worked near the canal.

"There!"

Gary pointed his torch at the square patch of dirty grey surrounded by boards and "keep out" signs.

"I was going by and thought I heard a noise, so I

shone my torch into it," Needy said. "That's when I saw it. Look." Gary couldn't see anything.

"Saw what?" Ben asked, staring at the area that Ted had pointed to.

"The body," Ted said. "A girl, it looked like, sinking in the concrete. Can't you make out the shape?" Now he pointed it out, Gary could kind of see a silhouette, or rather, a few lines, where something had sunk.

"A young girl, you say?"

"I didn't get a good look. The body was halfway under when I got here."

"You're sure she was dead?" Gary again.

"If she wasn't then, she is now. I saw her head go under, and it's been five minutes." Ben was on the radio, calling for assistance.

"You'd better get a move on," Ted told them. "It's slow drying, but, by morning, that stuff'll be set. You'll have one hell of a job getting her out!"

This wasn't Chicago in the twenties. Nobody knew what to do about a corpse encrusted in cement. If it hadn't been for Ted, the body would never have been discovered. Whoever dumped it knew what they were doing. The corpse would probably be a casualty of a drug fracas. The city had plenty of young girls on the game: runaways from the city's children's homes, half of them, living with pushers or supporting a pimp's drug habit, their lives as disposable as a used syringe.

Time was of the essence. A site manager was found, then a foreman. Floodlights were sent for. The foreman reckoned that they could probably dig the area around the body out before the cement completely set. An expert called in from Forensics was unhappy about this, arguing that the digger they used to retrieve the body might damage the remains so badly that the police would never be able to establish cause of death.

"The stuff was poured just after four," the foreman told CID. "Last thing we did before knocking off. The body must have been put in within two hours of that, or it wouldn't have sunk, specially if it's a slight girl, like the nightwatchman says."

Ben and Gary were relieved just before midnight, by which time the police were nowhere near getting the body out, and the concrete had completely set.

16

"Young lady waiting for someone from CID," said the front desk officer as Neil got in early. He'd not slept after Melanie woke him up, had spent most of the night walking the streets, trying to think of a way to get over her or get her back.

"Name?"

"She wouldn't give it. Says it's about Mark Murray. Interview room one's free." It would be, at this time of day. Scarcely eight. Most of the morning shift would be skiving off, having some breakfast. It was too early for crime. This time on a Saturday, you might get called for an alarm accidentally going off, or householders waking up to find that they'd been burgled. You didn't get witnesses suddenly deciding to come forward.

"Hear about the concrete body?" the desk officer called after Neil, but he was already introducing himself to the girl. She was a slim, attractive seventeen year old. Her name was Lori James.

"There was this appeal on Radio Trent," she told Neil. "People who were outside the radio station on Wednesday, just before Mark Murray was murdered."

"Thanks for coming in," Neil said. "I appreciate it. This won't take long."

"My parents won't have to know, will they?"

"Not if you don't want them to," Neil promised. "But why shouldn't they know that you were there, getting an autograph? Skiving off school, were you?"

"It's a bit more embarrassing than that."

"Tell me."

Lori explained that she'd had last lesson free at her sixth-form college, so popped into town to go shopping. She'd had a personal stereo with her and was listening to the Mark Murray interview on Radio Trent.

"I was outside Marks and Sparks and I realized that Radio Trent was just up the road on Castlegate. The interview was ending, so I wandered over there. You see, I knew Mark, a little. I didn't suppose he'd remember me, but my brother Warren used to hang out with him and I had the heaviest crush on him when I was eleven. So I thought I'd pass by and say 'hello' if I bumped into him. But there were half a dozen other girls there. I would have left but, just then, he came out."

"Did he recognize you?" Neil asked.

"No. He started signing autographs for the other girls, who were younger, except for one, and she also hung back. Then he noticed me and said hello. I told him who I was and he asked after Warren and then…" Her face went red.

"What?" Neil asked. "Something personal? Look, I can get a woman officer if…"

"It's OK," Lori said, embarrassment crossing her face. "It's only … I'd gone along on a whim and two minutes later, there was Mark suggesting that I go to bed with him, as though it were the most natural thing in the world. He told me his room number and the name of his hotel, said the door would be open."

"And you said you'd go?" Neil asked.

"I didn't say that I wouldn't. But, actually, I had no idea where the hotel was and, you know, I've got a boyfriend. I wouldn't cheat on him, no matter how famous Mark is … was."

"I see. Tell me, do you read the *Evening Post*?"

"Not often, no."

Neil thought about what she'd said. It seemed that this girl, not Tamara Crane, was the one who Mark Murray had propositioned. Yet how did Tamara know what Mark had said to Lori? And, if

Tamara really was the killer, how did she know that Lori had not gone to the hotel?

"What did you do next, after he'd propositioned you?"

"Mark returned to signing autographs. He seemed to expect me to go, so I went. But not to his hotel."

"Where?"

"To the Market Square. I caught a bus home."

"Did anyone follow you?"

"Not that I noticed."

"How about when Mark spoke to you," Neil asked, "was there anyone else within earshot?" Lori thought for a moment. "There was a middle-aged bloke. I think he was Radio Trent security, or something. I didn't pay much attention to him. And another girl about my age. She left when I did."

"What did she look like?"

Lori described a familiar figure. Neil showed her a photograph of Tamara Crane. "That's her, yes."

"This girl, did you tell her that you weren't going back to Mark's room?"

"No. I didn't speak to her at all."

"Are you sure she heard what Mark said?"

"Oh yes, she was very close by."

"You didn't speak to her?"

"No. I left."

"But the girl could have followed you?"

"I suppose."

"She'd have heard Mark say the room number?"

"Yes."

"All right," Neil said. "You've been extremely helpful. Thank you. I'd appreciate it if you didn't talk to the press. There are one or two details you've given us that could make all the difference."

"I won't talk to anyone else," Lori said. "All those horrible stories about Mark in the papers yesterday. I don't want to add to them."

She obviously hadn't seen that morning's papers. All of the tabloids had Tamara Crane's picture plastered across their covers. Many labelled their story "exclusive" even though the local evening paper had beaten them to it by eighteen hours.

In a way, Neil realized, Lori's story confirmed Tamara Crane's confession. She could be telling the truth about having killed Murray after all. Tamara had overheard him chatting up Lori, followed her to the bus, then gone up to Mark's room in her place. It would explain why Mark hadn't recognized Tamara. But if she was the real killer, why had the girl spun such a confusing tale?

"What was that you were saying about a concrete body?" he asked the desk officer.

Dylan got to the station at nine, joining Greasby and Neil, who told him about his interview with Lori James.

"We should take nothing for granted," the DI

said. "It could be that Crane's a flake and we're barking up the wrong tree by looking at Mark Murray's past. Now Anna Derbyshire's disappeared, too. This might not be about Murray, it might be about the play."

"You're suggesting that somebody didn't like their performances?" Dylan quipped. "Or maybe this is some kind of publicity stunt for Trudy Runcible?"

"I don't know what I'm suggesting. So trawl for anything, no matter how obscure. I don't want anyone interviewing the same cast member as on Wednesday night. Neil, take Lynda Crabbe and the other actress, Pamela Traynor. Chris, take Jeremy Eaton and Paul Santiago. I'll speak to the hotel manager and whatshisname, Geoff Darlington."

Neil gave Dylan a lift. As they drove to the hotel, he talked about the body found the night before.

"A concrete coffin, huh? I didn't realize we had the mafia in Nottingham."

"The thing is," Neil said, "they've got to chip the stuff off. The autopsy could take days. In the meantime, nobody's sure what's in there. The nightwatchman thought it looked like a young woman, but the light wasn't good and..."

"You don't think that..." Dylan started to say, then shut up. Anna Derbyshire was missing, but she was hardly a girl. Also, the way the body was dumped suggested the involvement of professional criminals. Neil went on.

"We're probably talking about dental records to identify her. Presuming it is a her."

They parked outside the Smith Square Hotel. There were several new wreaths around the hotel entrance. As often as the hotel staff moved them, not wanting the place associated with death, fans brought along new ones, which the guests had to step around. The CID officers went inside.

Reluctantly, Dylan walked past Lynda Crabbe's room. He would have liked to explain that he hadn't been fibbing about the kids, that he really would like to see her again and maybe, when he got off duty … but Jeremy Eaton was expecting him. The actor had been transferred to a bigger room the night before. He was still in his dressing gown and had a new, expensive-looking haircut.

"Not interviewing Lynda?" he asked, with a grin which showed that he knew exactly what Chris had been up to the night before last.

"Not today. I'm here to see if you remember anything else about what happened on Wednesday."

"Not really," Eaton said. "Like I told the other bloke, I was asleep."

"Tell me again," Dylan said.

Eaton had no alibi worth speaking of, but wasn't a serious suspect. True, he benefited from Murray's death, but actors didn't go round topping each other, then show up on stage the same night. Not in real life, anyway, not as far as Chris was concerned.

He went through the details with Eaton one more time, stressing the strange people in the hotel angle: someone must have seen something that Wednesday afternoon. But he drew a blank.

Paul Santiago was no help either. He seemed more concerned about Anna Derbyshire than Mark Murray.

"What do you think's happened to her? Shouldn't you issue some kind of alert, get people looking for her?"

"We don't want to start a scare. And we've no reason to suspect foul play."

"Then where do you think she's gone?"

"I don't know," Dylan admitted. "Have you any ideas?"

Santiago became earnest. "I can think of two possibilities. Either whoever murdered Mark had it in for Anna, too. Or Anna was responsible for Mark's death and decided to get away before she was caught. Both seem rather … extreme."

"They do," Dylan agreed, "but killing someone is pretty *extreme* too." He had yet to come up with a theory which made any sense at all.

When he'd finished with Santiago, Dylan checked that the coast was clear and knocked on Lynda Crabbe's door. Luckily, her interview was over.

"I wasn't expecting to see you," she said. "I thought you said…"

"Had to work overtime. The kids are staying with their mother."

"I'll bet she's pissed off with you."

"To put it mildly," Chris admitted. "By the way, I thought you'd like to know, one of the ushers recognized you from the early showing of the movie on Wednesday. So your alibi's sound."

"I always knew that," Lynda said. "But I'm glad that you do too."

"I was thinking, if you're not doing anything … I was wondering whether we could meet up after the show tonight?"

"I'd like that, yes. Wait for me in the bar? I should be there just after ten."

"That'd be great."

"You haven't got time to stay for a drink now, have you?"

"Well," he said, looking at his watch and guessing that Neil and the DI were probably doing more thorough interviews than he had. "Maybe a quick one."

17

Ben spent Saturday morning in bed with Julie and the *Independent* newspaper. At one, Curt knocked on the door.

"There's this friend of Natalie's here. Jo. She wants a word with Ben."

"I meant to tell you about her," Julie said, as Ben got up.

"Tell me what?"

"Oh, judge for yourself. It sounded like a made-up story to me."

The two girls were waiting in the kitchen. Natalie looked her age, a waif-like fourteen-year-old with short hair and an awkwardness about her. Her friend looked nearer sixteen. Yet, as it turned out, she was from Natalie's year at school.

"This is Jo," Natalie said. "I thought she ought to have a word with you."

"What about?" Ben asked.

"Mark Murray."

"Tell me," Ben turned to the girl with the long blonde hair.

"There was a big story in yesterday's paper about this girl who confessed to killing him."

"Yes, I know." Ben didn't have anything to do with the Mark Murray case, hadn't been following it closely, though it was the talk of the station. He knew the basics of Tamara Crane's confession.

"I don't know if she killed him or not, but part of her story's a lie."

"Which part?"

"She says she showed him the way to this restaurant after the play on Wednesday night, but she didn't. I did."

"I see. So…?"

"If she's lying about that…" Jo began, but Ben interrupted her.

"Weren't CID appealing for people who saw Mark that night to come forward?"

"Yes, but…"

"Nobody believed Jo at school," Natalie interrupted. "So she thought that the police wouldn't either. Then she told me all about it. They had a long conversation…"

"I can remember everything we said," Jo told

him. "I wrote it all down in my diary. He confided in me."

"Confided in a fourteen-year-old girl who he'd never met before?" Ben asked, somewhat incredulous, though the girl didn't look like a fantasist.

"I know what you mean," Jo said, "but he seemed to like me."

"If you say so. OK." Ben got up. "I'll ring CID, find out if they're interested in what you've got." He called the police switchboard and got himself put through to the incident room. The answering machine was switched on. Ben thought about leaving a message, but he was due on duty in an hour.

"No one there," he said, putting the phone down. "Still, you've already waited two days, it can wait another hour."

When he got to the station, Ben poked his head into the CID incident room, where Dylan, Greasby and Clare were in conference.

"Sorry to interrupt, but I've got a teenage girl downstairs, says she knows something about Mark Murray."

"Plonk her in reception," Greasby told him, not even looking round. "I'll send someone down there when there's time. So, what are we looking for?"

"The girl who walked him to the restaurant," Clare said.

"The woman he met there," Chris put in.

"And, most of all, Anna Derbyshire," Greasby said, as Ben shut the door behind him.

"Someone will be down in a while," he told Jo, leaving her in the shabby waiting area. As he hurried to start his shift, a familiar figure breezed in. Seeing Ben, he froze for a moment, then put on his signature, sleazy smile. Ian Jagger.

"Constable. I hope there are no hard feelings?" Ben stared at the solicitor, wondering what the hell he was talking about. Seven or eight months had passed since the Jed Sutcliffe affair. That was when Jagger had emerged spotless from a series of nasty racial incidents which he had – partially, at least – orchestrated. Then Jagger had added insult to injury by employing Charlene, Ben's ex, as his token black worker. That move neatly stopped the media casting aspersions of racism on him. So it was a bit late to discuss hard feelings and, anyway, there were some things you couldn't forgive. Jagger was an evil, tricky sod, and Ben meant to get him, if he ever had the chance. Ignoring the man's words, he kept walking towards the parade room.

"I'm sorry to interrupt. I was told to come through." Clare looked up to see Ian Jagger walk into the incident room, looking as though he owned the place.

"I don't know how to put this," said the solicitor. "It's my client…"

"She wants to retract her confession?" Clare suggested. Jagger, for once in his life, looked embarrassed. "As a matter of fact, she does."

Greasby sat Jagger down. Clare could hardly hold the fake confession against the solicitor. They'd all had their doubts, but a solicitor had to take his or her clients' word about what happened.

"What's the story?" Greasby enquired. Jagger told it succinctly. "It seems that Ms Crane's motive for confessing was to blacken Mark Murray's name. Now she's succeeded in doing that, there's no point in her staying in custody. It seems that she invented a fabric of lies and half-truths which, on first inspection, appeared credible. I must stress to you that, while my partner and I had our suspicions, we had to accept our clients' protestations of guilt. This is a disturbed young woman, deeply concerned by the fate of her sister. However, if you wish to charge her with wasting police time..."

"You know what the policy is," Greasby told him, curtly. Tamara had wasted well over a hundred hours of police time and ought to be prosecuted, Clare knew. But she remembered Phoenix, the arsonist who had done far worse things than Tamara, yet whom Jagger had managed to keep out of prison. He'd probably do the same for Tamara Crane.

"Will you be releasing her?" Jagger asked.

"Maybe," Greasby told him. "I'll have to look

into a few things first. After all, the fact that she's changed her mind doesn't mean that her confession's false. She may merely have decided that she doesn't want to go to prison."

"True," Jagger said, "but I should warn you that she has an alibi which she previously concealed. Directly after seeing Murray at Radio Trent, Tamara walked to the station and caught the next train home to Norwich. Her mother met her at the other end. I'm sure we can find other witnesses if we need to."

"So the mother must have known that it was a lie too," Greasby snapped. "Maybe they planned this little hoax together. We ought to do her as well."

"I'm sorry," Jagger repeated. "I think we've all been played for fools."

"Sounds like it," Greasby said. "You can tell Tamara that we'll be reinterviewing her later."

"When would that be? Only I have a…"

"*When I'm ready*," Greasby said, no longer hiding the anger in his voice. "Until then, let her stew. I'll give you notice."

"Thanks," Jagger said. "I appreciate it. Tell me, do you have other suspects?"

"I can't tell you that."

"Just out of curiosity, did Murray leave a will?"

"If he did, we haven't found it yet," Greasby told him.

"He must have been a very wealthy young man,"

Jagger commented. He was turning to leave when the Detective Superintendent walked in. It wasn't like her to show up on a weekend unless there was big news.

"I thought you lot ought to be the first to know," she told Greasby. "Forensics have just been in touch. They've identified the body found in the cement last night from her dental records. The deceased is Anna Derbyshire, an actress, aged twenty-six. Cause of death: strangulation, though she had sleeping pills in her system too. Her body was weighted with bricks from the building site. And she was two months pregnant."

It was only when she'd finished that the Superintendent noticed the solicitor. Ian Jagger shook her hand. They were obviously old pals.

"At least that's one murder we can be sure my client didn't commit," he said.

18

Anna Derbyshire's death changed everything. The likelihood was that they were looking for a double killer now. Trudy Runcible had moved up the suspect list and Tamara Crane was probably in the clear. Scotland Yard were phoned and asked to recheck Runcible's alibi for Mark Murray's murder.

Trudy was still in Nottingham. Neil called and asked her to come to the station. Maybe the playwright had pulled the wool over Neil's eyes. Or maybe the solution was more obvious. Who directly benefited from Mark and Anna's deaths? Only two people: Jeremy Eaton and Lynda Crabbe. Eaton's alibi was non-existent. Who had checked Lynda Crabbe's alibi? Dylan – he'd found a witness who saw her at the cinema, and seemed to think that she was all right. Also, if Eaton and Crabbe were working together, wouldn't they have alibied each other, rather than leaving themselves wide open? Neil couldn't be sure. He ought to have an instinct for stuff like this. Sometimes, he thought that he wasn't a natural detective.

Neil looked at the list of suspects which Chris Dylan had written on the whiteboard on Thursday afternoon. He crossed Anna Derbyshire off it. As things stood, CID still had a huge list of suspects, but no evidence against anyone whatsoever.

A woman did it, that was Neil's inclination. The way Murray was killed – hit with a heavy object from behind – that was a woman's way of killing. Strangulation, sleeping pills, that sounded like a woman too. But who? The phone rang before he could formulate any answers whatsoever. It was one of the officers from Major Crimes.

"Just bringing you up to speed on our missing people. Gillian Crane, still no word. As for Mark Murray's father, we've confirmed that he's emigrated to Australia, lives near Melbourne. We haven't managed to get in touch with him yet. I take it you've heard about Anna Derbyshire?"

"Yes," Neil said. "What're the chances of finding out who the baby's father is?"

"We'll be able to get a DNA sample from the foetus. Not that it'll tell us much unless the baby's

Mark Murray's – or somebody else whose DNA we've got on record."

"When will you know?"

"Things are slow because of the weekend, but we're talking about tomorrow morning at the latest."

"Thanks." Neil went back to the whiteboard, trying to think of new names to add to the list of suspects, or apply new logic to the names that were already there. There was something missing, some little piece of information that would provide CID with the break they needed. But he had no idea where that information was going to come from.

"Clare! Back in harness, I see."

"Hello, sir." Clare had wanted to avoid Tony Winter, the inspector who was in charge of her shift and several others, partly because she knew what his next question would be.

"When are you rejoining us?"

"As soon as CID are finished with me."

"You don't look too busy now. Sure you're not putting off being back on the beat? There's nothing like good exercise to get your ankle back to full fitness."

"I'm sure you're right, Sir, but…" Clare was tired. She had been at work until twelve, then back at eight, and had hardly slept in between. Now, if she wasn't careful, the inspector would have her back in uniform, pounding a beat until ten tonight. However, that didn't turn out to be what he wanted.

"Ben Shipman brought a girl in over an hour ago. She's got some information about Mark Murray. Is someone going to see her?" Clare looked around. The other officers were dealing with the flurry of enquiries which had arisen from the identification of Anna Derbyshire. Clare was here to answer the phone. They had all been too busy to remember the girl that Ben had brought in. Should Clare wait for a more senior officer? Why bother? It was unlikely that the girl had anything important.

"I'll come and talk to her myself, Sir," Clare said, switching the answering machine on.

Jo McCord looked fifteen or sixteen, but turned out to be fourteen. She explained that she was one of the fans waiting outside the Theatre Royal the night before Mark was murdered.

"But I went to a different exit. I thought he might try to sneak out, and I was right. At five to ten, the door opened and there was this security guy, letting him out. Mark was asking about where some restaurant was and I said that I knew."

"Did you?"

"Sort of. I'd been there with my mum and dad once. So I said I'd show him. It wasn't far. Though, actually…" She looked mildly embarrassed.

"Actually what?" Clare asked.

"I didn't so much get lost as take the long way round. We were talking, and he didn't seem to mind. We had a long conversation about all sorts of things." The girl was probably making it up, Clare guessed, another crazy fan. The story about the girl who walked Murray to the restaurant had finally found its way into the papers that morning, leaked in the hope that she would come forward. But one crucial piece of information had been deliberately omitted.

"You eventually found the restaurant?"

"Yes."

"And what happened then?"

"He went in." So that was it, Clare thought, a fake. But she had to make sure.

"Did nothing happen before he went in?"

This time, Jo clearly blushed. "Umm…"

"You must tell me," Clare said.

"I … uh, asked him for a kiss."

"And did he give you one?" She nodded. "In front of the restaurant?"

"No, we went round the side so we couldn't be seen from the street." Big mistake, Clare knew. The woman who Mark was meeting had seen them, as had Penelope Palmer. But her heart was racing. It looked like this girl was genuine after all.

"How long did he kiss you for?"

"I can't tell," Jo told her. "It felt like for ever but

it might have only been five minutes." Penelope Palmer had said two.

"He was fantastic," Jo said, her eyes watering. "I've never been kissed like that before."

"I want to thank you for coming in," Clare said, handing the girl a tissue. "And I want you to try and remember everything that Mark said to you that night. Do you think you can do that?"

"Oh yes," Jo said. "I wrote down every word in my diary as soon as I got home."

Tears ran down Trudy Runcible's face. Her storm of red hair was tied back, and she'd dressed in black, as if anticipating the news that the police had just given her. Trudy didn't seem to realize that she was a suspect. Neil wasn't sure that she was one. He couldn't see how she'd have managed to kill her lover, hide the body for over a day, then know where to dump it. Nevertheless, tough questions had to be asked, and DI Greasby was asking them.

"You say you were at a party the night that Anna disappeared. Can you give me details?"

"I only stopped by for an hour or so. It was at the Groucho Club. Very busy."

"But people will remember seeing you there?"

"I expect so. Though everyone was pretty much off their heads by the time I arrived."

"What made you late?"

"I'd been writing all day, trying to get the last act

of my play rewritten. I had to workshop it the next day. That's what you walked in on." The *you* she was referring to was Neil. But Trudy had just revealed that she had no alibi for the day that Anna disappeared. She could have driven to Nottingham, killed Anna, hidden the body, then got back in time for the party. Greasby nodded at Neil.

"Trudy, you don't mind me asking, do you, was Anna exclusively gay?" So far, they had held back the information about her pregnancy. If Trudy was guilty, it probably provided her motive.

"Since she was twenty-one, yes. Before that, she was somewhat … confused, or so she told me. Can you tell me what makes this relevant?"

"We have to look into every angle," Greasby said.

"I'm sorry if this is embarrassing," Neil said, feeling bloody embarrassed himself, "but do you mind telling me, were you and Anna … monogamous?"

"Yes, completely." Not as completely as you believe, unfortunately, Neil thought. But the next stage of questioning had better wait until they had the result of the DNA tests. Neil looked at the DI with a shrug in his eyes.

"I'm sorry we had to put you through this," Greasby told the playwright. "But time is of the essence. We may have to come back to you with more questions."

"Whatever you need to find the killer," Runcible

told them. "Do you think that this is connected with Mark's murder?"

"It seems likely," Greasby said. "But we know nothing for sure." The inspector was right, Neil thought, as he showed Trudy out. Three days after the first murder and they knew nothing. Tomorrow, the travelling company left Nottingham. The trail would soon go cold.

19

Mark Murray seemed edgy at first, worried about something. He asked Jo her name, where she went to school and what she thought of the play. Then he went quiet and, when she asked him whether he missed being on the telly, didn't reply. So she wittered on about how good he used to be and how she used to tape the episodes and watch them again and again, fast forwarding to the bits that he was in.

"I can't believe I'm standing next to you now," she finished, and the actor smiled his famous shy smile.

It had rained a lot that day, and the pavement glistened beneath the streetlights.

"Is something wrong?" Jo got up the nerve to ask.

"I'm sorry," he said. "I'm not being very good company, am I? Thing is, I'm going to meet somebody. An old girlfriend. I haven't seen her for a couple of years and … she's got a lot of reasons to dislike me. I'm not looking forward to it."

"Why are you going, then?" Jo asked. Surely, if you were famous, you could do exactly what you wanted to do.

"Because she asked me. It's funny, I've heard nothing from her in all this time, not even a Christmas card, then she sends a note to me at the theatre." Jo left a silence there, to see if he had anything to add. A student walked by and, as she passed them, seemed to recognize Mark. She turned back and stared, but Mark didn't notice. Probably he was used to it.

"God knows what she wants," he went on, suddenly. "When you become well known, it gets like everybody wants something off you: money, friendship, an introduction, or an autograph." Jo decided then and there not to ask for an autograph. Instead, she asked him what all the magazines she read were unable to tell her.

"Have you got a steady girlfriend now?"

"Interested in the position?" Mark responded. Jo giggled, which wasn't the coolest thing to do, but he giggled too, so it was OK.

"Truth is," he told her, "I'm not a one woman man. I suppose it sounds selfish, but, I like women a lot and, right now, I can have as many girlfriends as I want. Why should I restrict myself to one?"

"You might fall in love with her," Jo said, tentatively.

"*Love*," Mark said mockingly. "You wouldn't believe how often women say they're *in love* with me – sometimes when I've only known them a few days. It's a kind of blackmail, as far as I can tell. A trick. Have you ever been in love?"

"No," Jo admitted.

"Me neither. So I don't know whether *love* exists or not. Maybe when I'm older, more mature, I'll meet someone I want to start a family with. But I'd have to be sure. My dad left home when I was five. I wouldn't wish that on any kid.

"But we've been talking about me for ages," Mark went on. "That's what people like me do. We talk about ourselves all the time until we forget that other people exist. Sometimes, I do so many interviews, I don't think I'm real any more. Let's talk about you. Are your parents still together?"

"Yes."

"You're lucky. Got a boyfriend?"

"Nah," Jo admitted.

"Not ready yet?" Mark asked, adding flirt-atiously, "I can't believe you don't get offers."

She spoke hesitantly. "I've been out with boys, older ones, but the ones who ask me, they only want one thing, and when you won't give it to them, they lose interest. And the ones I really like – you know, the ones who I might like to … you know, with – eventually – they're the ones who are too shy to ask me out."

"They won't always be too shy," Mark told her, kindly. "If you can't wait, you could always ask them."

"*Ask them!* You're kidding."

"No. Believe me. You only get things in this world by asking. Go up to the person, be nice, say *I really want this job* or *I think you're really nice, would you like to go out sometime?* What's the worst thing they can say? No."

"And if they do say no, I'd be crushed." The conversation was getting really interesting, but they were coming up to the restaurant. Jo thought about taking another diversion, but didn't want to be so sneaky when Mark was being so real. The actor kept talking.

"You might be crushed the first time, but it gets easier. They say that the things you end up regretting aren't the things you did, but the things you didn't do. The people you should have asked out, the break you should have at least tried for. So, the guy turns you down – maybe he's seeing someone else at the moment. But you might move on to his reserve list. You know what the most attractive thing is in another person?"

"No. What?"

"Them being attracted to you. If you know that somebody wants you, you're more inclined to find them attractive."

"Does that work with you?" Jo asked.

"Oh, I dunno," Mark said, looking at the restaurant. "Is this it?"

"Yes." She thought that he was bound to go straight in, but he finished answering her question.

"When *everybody* seems to want you, your interest wanes. You're more interested in the ones who don't want you. Stars are often like that, I've heard. They want the whole world to love them, even the people they can't stand."

"Weird," Jo said. Mark shrugged and gave her a goofy smile.

"People *are* weird," he said, holding out his hand. "They're not always what they seem. You can never be quiet sure where they're coming from." He held out his hand. Instead of shaking it, Jo took his earlier words to heart, decided to be brave.

"Giverchisspl," she'd said, the words coming out wrong.

"Pardon," he said, giving her *that* smile, the one she'd freeze-framed so many times.

"Give us a kiss, please," she'd repeated, not garbling the words this time. As she prayed for a peck on the cheek, Mark took a quick glance through the restaurant window.

"What, with the world watching?" She thought

he was turning her down, but he took her hand, holding it, not shaking it, and guided her round the corner, beside the bay window.

"It was a proper kiss," Jo told the constable. "It seemed to last ages. I couldn't believe it. I don't expect you to. I haven't told any of my friends, not even Natalie. They'd think I was making the whole thing up. You do, don't you?"

The detective shook her head. "No I don't. I wasn't sure whether to believe you until you told me that. But you were seen kissing Murray. That's how I know that the rest of what you're saying's true, too. A couple more questions before I pass your inform- ation on," Clare said. "The woman he was meeting. Did he tell you her name?" Jo tried to dredge her memory. Yes, there had been a name, but mumbled, so she hadn't heard it properly, and hadn't put it in her diary. The police woman waited patiently.

"I think – I'm not sure, but I think – he might have said Gill. Or Gillian."

"Gill Crane?"

"He didn't say a second name. He might have said her name was Gill."

"Thanks," the DC said, holding out her hand. "You've been incredibly helpful, Jo. Thanks so much for coming forward."

"Will this help to catch whoever murdered him?"

"Yes. I really think it might. We'll probably ask

you to keep quiet about what you've told us for the time being. And a more senior detective will want to interview you. Do you mind hanging around?"

"Not if it'll help catch whoever killed Mark." The detective got up and left the interview room. As the door swung back, Jo saw her step into the corridor, her brisk walk quickly turning into a run.

20

The deadline for the Sunday newspapers was four-thirty on Saturday afternoon, half an hour away. There were rumours that Tamara Crane had retracted her confession and the police were no longer treating her as a serious suspect. The press smelt blood. All officers were under instructions not to confirm the story. Maybe, by tomorrow, they would have a new suspect. At ten past four, the press officer got through to Chris Dylan for the third time that afternoon.

"I've just had a call from the *Mail*. They've heard a whisper that the body found last night was Anna Derbyshire. Has one of your lot leaked it?"

"No," Chris assured her. "More likely to be Trudy Runcible." He couldn't think who else knew.

The press would have a field day now that Derbyshire was dead. Chris could see the headlines: *Former Child Star in Lesbian Love Nest. Pregnant and Murdered!* Or something like that – Chris had never been very good at English.

"The superintendent isn't going to like it," Chris was told.

"Did you deny it?" he asked the Press Officer.

"No, I said I'd call them back."

"Don't. We could do with a day's grace before the media circus gets worse."

"The Sundays won't let go. It'll be old news by next week. Do you want to turn this around, appeal for witnesses who saw the body being dumped?"

"Try it if you like," Chris said. "But don't let on who the body is. Got to go." He hung up. Let someone else deal with the vultures from the press. He wanted this day to be over, but he'd be lucky to finish before ten, when he was meeting the lovely Lynda Crabbe.

Who had killed Anna Derbyshire? Chris wouldn't be able to make an educated guess until they found out who the father of her baby was. He was trying to track down Jeremy Eaton, the most likely member of the cast after Mark Murray. Anna Derbyshire had been on tour for two months. It seemed a fair bet that the father was one of the four men associated with it. Anna had denied sleeping with Mark Murray. That left Eaton, Darlington and

Santiago. The latter two had already agreed to give DNA samples, without knowing why. But Eaton was out somewhere. Neil was trying to track him down.

"Chris, I've got news!" It was a breathless Clare Coppola, running into the room.

"Where is everybody?" she asked.

"Out doing detective work," Chris told her.

"Then you need to get them here. I think I know who killed Mark Murray!"

"It's happening for me," Jeremy told Steve. "So it can certainly happen for you. You're better looking than Mark was. Probably a better actor, too. It's a case of hanging in there, waiting for the breaks." He passed the joint back to Steve, in whose Forest Fields flat they were sitting. Jeremy was celebrating, having just heard that he'd got a part in a docu-drama Central were making about the motorway team, a bunch of big-time burglars who were currently waiting to be tried. Jeremy was to play Joe, the eighteen-year-old burglar who had accidentally caused three members of the team to be caught.

"Maybe you could give me a break," Steve suggested, jokingly. "Call in sick while we're performing in Newcastle. Give me a chance to show what I can do."

"Dream on," Jeremy said, as the doorbell rang.

Probably Sam, Steve's girlfriend. He passed the joint back to Jeremy and went down to let her in. Opening the door, he realized that he'd made a mistake.

"Steve," Neil Foster said, "sorry to interrupt your Saturday afternoon, but we heard that you were pally with Jeremy Eaton and wondered whether he was with you."

"Well, uh…"

"This is really important," said the detective inspector who was with Neil.

"He's upstairs." They followed him up. Greasby frowned at the narcotic smell in the room, but neither he nor Neil mentioned it.

"Mr Eaton," Greasby said. "We'd be grateful if you'd accompany us to the station where a police doctor can take a blood sample. We're testing all the male members of your company in order to eliminate them from our enquiries."

"Now?" Jeremy blustered, "I have to perform tonight. Losing blood might affect my…"

"Doesn't stop you smoking that stuff, does it?" Greasby snarled, pointing at the ash tray. "Only a pin-prick, I promise. But we need you straight away."

They took Eaton with them. He must be a suspect, Steve realized. Suppose they tested Jeremy's blood and found that he was the one who'd killed Mark Murray? Steve might get his own break at the Theatre Royal tonight.

* * *

"It's Gill Crane," Clare said. "It's got to be her!" The ex-girlfriend roughly matched the description that Penelope Palmer had given of the woman who Mark met in the restaurant. This, combined with the name, was too big a coincidence for it not to be her.

"It's helpful," Chris Dylan said, "but hardly definite."

"If Gill Crane's still alive and has nothing to hide she'd have come forward by now," Clare argued. "We've been appealing for the woman in the restaurant."

Dylan didn't agree. "We charged her sister with the murder, remember? The press said that Gill had probably killed herself. So, presumably, Gill Crane – if it is her – has plenty of reasons for wanting to stay incognito. Still, whatever name she's using, we should be able to find her quickly now that we know she's in the area." They began making calls, interrupting them to bring Neil and John Greasby up to speed. Clare reminded them of Ian Jagger's last comment, about Mark's will.

"Mark must have been worth a lot of money. That could be motive enough for murder."

"There's no will that we know of," Greasby said. "So, unless Mark turns out to have children, his parents will split the proceeds."

"The father's meant to be no good," Neil commented.

"And we wouldn't even bother to investigate him," Chris added. "Living in Australia's a convincing enough alibi."

"Doesn't explain who killed Derbyshire, though, does it?" Greasby said.

"Maybe the two killings aren't connected." Chris.

"Pull the other one." Greasby.

A phone rang before they could discuss it further. Dylan spoke for a minute then turned to the others.

"Ted Murray's still in Australia."

"Have the Melbourne police actually seen him?" Neil.

"No need," Greasby said. "He's in Adelaide, serving seven years for fraud."

There was no press conference to mark Tamara Crane's release. News of Anna Derbyshire's death had been leaked and the reporters – with a deadline minutes away – had moved on to that story. The news of Tamara's innocence wouldn't be in the papers until Monday, when, hopefully, her arrest would be swiftly forgotten. Ian Jagger had insisted on going to collect Tamara himself. Charlene didn't see why. It would do the firm's reputation no good, being seen to represent crazy kids who confessed to murders they didn't commit.

In the end, however, Ian couldn't go. Another

case demanded his attention. He gave his fiancé strict instructions.

"Don't let her talk to any press. And don't take anything she has to say too seriously." These were Ian's last words before rushing off to see a magistrate who'd indecently exposed himself in Victoria Park.

There weren't any press waiting. The train timetable didn't allow Tamara's mother to get to Nottingham in time to meet her. So it was just Charlene. While waiting for Tamara to be released, she bumped into Clare.

"How about that drink?" she said, being friendly, for she had always liked Clare. She had more about her than most of the other plods who Ben worked with.

"Sure. After work one day next week?"

"Whatever suits you."

"Better make it Monday," Clare said. "I might be back on the beat by Tuesday." They arranged to meet at around six in the Playhouse bar.

"I'm waiting for Tamara Crane," Charlene explained. "Any idea if you're going to charge her with wasting police time?"

"I don't suppose there'll be a decision until we've charged the real killer." Something didn't feel right, Charlene decided as Clare went off. Ian, she knew, had leaked Anna Derbyshire's death in order to take the heat off Tamara. This was a sneaky tactic, but hardly a reprehensible one. The media were bound to find out within a few hours anyhow. Charlene's fiancé had, however, been increasingly secretive about this case. Ian always liked to play things close to his chest. Now that they were living together, practically married, shouldn't he become more open? Yet why would Ian break the habits of a life-time?

Tamara Crane came out of her cell looking pale and sullen.

"They've dropped the charges then," she said.

"Yes," Charlene said, smiling comfortingly.

"Your boss is a really clever man," Tamara said, staring at the floor.

"You're right. He is. But you're innocent. That's what counted the most." Tamara tried to give some kind of smile, failed. It must be awful, Charlene thought, having to spend two days in a cell. But not that awful. And Tamara had achieved her aim: she had blackened Mark Murray's name. The whole country now knew that he was a *sex-obsessed love cheat*.

"Are they going to charge me with the other thing?" Tamara wanted to know. "Wasting police time?"

"Maybe. They've got other things on their minds at the moment," Charlene explained. "There's been a second murder. Another actor in the play. So it looks like there's some kind of pattern." Tamara didn't seem terribly excited. She was in a kind of shock, Charlene guessed.

"Come on," she said to the girl. "I'll take you to the station." Someone ought to go with her on the train, but that wasn't Charlene's job. As she drove to the Midland Station, Tamara talked, almost to herself.

"I only did it for Gill, not for me." The girl should see a therapist, Charlene thought, as she drove into the short stay parking.

"I owed it to her. I couldn't live with myself if I hadn't done it."

"I think I understand," Charlene said, un-convincingly.

"Only now I can't live with myself anyway."

"Sorry?" Charlene asked, opening the car door for Tamara. "What was that?"

"You know something?" Tamara said, not answering directly but letting herself be led to the ticket counter. "He was the first and last. There won't be another."

"Mark Murray?" Charlene asked. The first and last what? The girl wasn't making sense.

"But he was so beautiful," Tamara went on. "So…"

Suddenly, it clicked. Charlene paid for the ticket, then, as they were walking down the stairs to the platform, she asked the question.

"Tamara, did you sleep with Mark Murray? Is

that why you confessed? Did you want to ruin Mark's reputation because you were guilty about sleeping with Gill's boyfriend?" Tamara looked at her coldly, saying nothing, *Don't take anything she has to say too seriously* Ian had said earlier. But Charlene wanted to know what had really happened. She wanted the world to make sense.

The train was nearly empty, but Tamara made no move to choose a seat. Charlene led her to one and sat her down.

"Your mum'll be waiting at the other end," she said, and was about to go when Tamara tugged at her sleeve. Charlene leant over. "What?"

"Your boss is a really clever man," Tamara said, repeating what she'd said at the police station.

"Why do you say that?" Charlene wanted to ask, but the guard began closing doors and she had to get off.

21

The Theatre Royal was less than a quarter full. Many ticket holders, hearing of the death of both stars, had not turned up. There were a few media vultures in the audience, on the off chance that a third cast member might be murdered, but there was nobody famous left on the stage. Geoff Darlington might have appeared regularly in *Casualty* and *Eastenders*, but he was hardly a household name.

The reporters all departed at the interval, no whiff of scandal to delay them. Chris Dylan took one of the vacated seats. He had spent most of the day with John Greasby, trying to track down Gill Crane. Chris had been sent to the theatre, not on account of his date with Lynda, which he had avoided mentioning, but to talk to Trudy Runcible. The playwright was in the Upper Circle, on the opposite side from him, watching the performances of the two new leads. Strange that she should be here, he thought, when her lover had been found dead the night before.

If Eaton hadn't done it, then Runcible was the best suspect. She had an alibi for Mark's murder, but maybe they could break that down. Maybe she had persuaded her actor buddies to cover for her, claiming that she was doing something she didn't want the police to know about, something short of murder. Working out where she was when Anna died was more difficult. Because of the condition of the body, Forensics couldn't pin down the time of Anna Derbyshire's death beyond six pm on Thursday to midday on Friday. No suspect could have a full alibi.

Trudy could have killed Anna and was the person most likely to have done so. It wasn't all that difficult to strangle someone, particularly if the victim was in a vulnerable position: asleep, for instance, after taking sleeping pills. Unfortunately, the effect of the cement made it impossible to find out the size of the hands which strangled Anna, only that death had probably been caused by hands, not wire or a cord.

So far, the police had avoided questioning Runcible again. The DI wanted to hold back the pregnancy revelation until it could be timed to maximum effect. Finally, though, Greasby had agreed to Chris confronting Trudy after the play. At least it would shake her up a little. Afterwards, she wouldn't be arrested, but kept under surveillance. Knowing that she was a suspect might lead Trudy to run, or to dispose of anything which could connect her with either murder.

Chris watched the play keenly, even though he'd seen it once before. Lynda was giving the part her all, confronting the corrupt politician with the disease she carried. The politician, undeterred, revealed to Lynda that she was really his daughter. The child she bore would be both his daughter and granddaughter. As Lynda screamed, Chris watched Trudy Runcible's reaction. She seemed moved. Chris wasn't. He couldn't think of these actors as the characters they were meant to be inhabiting. Until the case was closed, they were all suspects. Even Lynda, who he hoped to sleep with later tonight.

The play ended, to a brief ovation. As the audience left, Chris sat down next to Trudy.

"Would you mind waiting a minute? A couple of things I need to ask you."

"Sure," she said. "Why not?" There was resignation in her eyes. Maybe, Chris thought, she was ready to confess. He held back his excitement, trying to empathize with her, though empathy was a quality which few people would accuse him of possessing.

"We got the autopsy result. There was something you didn't tell us." Trudy showed no sign of surprise, or suspense, but Chris wanted *her* to tell *him*.

"Do you know what I mean?" he asked.

Trudy nodded slowly. "Anna was pregnant. We found out last Monday."

"*We?*"

"Yes. Our gynaecologist confirmed the test result. We had a big celebration before Anna caught the train to Nottingham."

"Celebration?"

"Yes. We'd been trying for a few weeks, since the donor agreed to…"

"The donor. So you did this…"

"Artificially," Trudy told him, bluntly. "Do you want me to go into details, or should I just give you the name of our gynaecologist? Logically, I should have had the babies, of course – having a baby gets in the way of acting more than it does writing. But I can't have kids. We tried."

"So the father…"

"It was Mark. He was so generous to Anna and me. All these people have called him a user, but he gave a lot to us. I didn't mention any of this before because I wanted to avoid the story getting out. Anna's family could live without all of the publicity." She paused. "Poor little baby. Was it a boy or a girl?"

"I don't know," Chris had to tell her.

"With Anna for a mother and Mark for a father, it would have been very beautiful, wouldn't it?"

"I'm sure it would."

"We were going to tell Mark the night that he … that he… And now all three of them are gone." She began to cry. Chris held her. After a while, she wiped her eyes and asked if it was OK for her to go. Chris saw Trudy to the door of the theatre, then, when she was out of sight, used his mobile phone to call off the surveillance. Next, he rang John Greasby with the news.

"Do you want me back there?" he finished.

"No. This is going nowhere. Neil and I are knocking off now. Get here about twelve tomorrow."

"Right you are." Chris made his way to the bar. The cast hadn't come in, with two exceptions. Steve Garrett was drinking with Lynda Crabbe. Steve was into older women, Chris knew. He thought for a moment that he'd blown his chance. But seeing Chris arrive, Steve left.

"See you in Newcastle on Monday," he told Lynda, who blew him a kiss.

"Saw the second half again," Chris commented, sitting down. "You were great."

"Thanks," Lynda said, giving him a kiss on the cheek. "Let me get you a drink."

"No, no, I'll get you one."

"I'll tell you what," she said, "why don't we go back to the hotel right now, order a bottle of champagne on room service, and drink it in bed?"

"Brilliant," Chris said, without conviction. For once, he didn't have any erotic impulses, his head still clouded with Trudy Runcible's double loss, which he couldn't tell Lynda about.

They walked through the city hand in hand. It was the usual wild Saturday night, but Lynda seemed to enjoy the shouting, running, jumping drunks, the swaying girls, shivering in their summer dresses. When Chris apologized for it, she said, "Think this is bad, you ought to see Newcastle on a Saturday night. Hey, maybe you could. Now I'm the leading lady, I should have a suite again. Want to come and stay with me next weekend?"

"Why not?" Chris said, and she kissed him again, on the lips this time. He had thought of him and Lynda as a one-night stand, but she seemed interested in more. And why not? A long distance relationship would suit Chris down to the ground. He could play the field here and Lynda wouldn't mind. His depression lifted. He squeezed her hand and kissed her again, feeling lucky.

22

Neil gave Clare a lift home and she invited him in for a drink. Clare was out of beer, but dug out the bottle of vodka which Ruth kept stashed in her room. She and Neil started by drinking the vodka with tonic and ice. Neil chose a tape to play, asked about her mum and dad. Later, when the tonic ran out, they took to drinking the vodka neat. It felt good. They discussed the two murders, but not for long. Neil was happy to move the conversation away from the job, to talk about more personal stuff. He mentioned something that Trudy Runcible had said to him, about not many men being drawn to powerful, intelligent women.

"But I am," he said. "Does that make me a wimp?"

"Probably," she told him, and they both laughed. Clare thought back to when they were going out and realized that she had always been in charge of their relationship. That was one of the main things wrong with it. Paul Grace had treated her as an equal, but he had always been the more experienced one. He had been much more important than her at work, and she had liked that. She tried to say some of this to Neil.

"Does that make me a sexual stereotype?" she asked. "Am I just pretending to be some kind of feminist when, really, I'm drawn to attractive, well-off men?"

"Don't ask me," Neil said. "At least Paul was only – what, thirty? Look at Charlene, marrying Jagger. He must be fifty."

"Forty-seven, according to the paper," Clare said. "I think she knows what she's doing. How did Ben take it?"

"I don't think anybody's dared to tell him yet."

"Then you ought to. You're his best mate."

"Am I?" Neil asked. "I suppose I still am."

"I'm glad that we can be mates again," Clare said, smiling and pouring out the rest of the vodka.

"Me too," Neil said. She put her glass down and sat next to Neil on the sofa, leaning her head on his shoulder. "This has been the longest, weirdest year of my life. I'll be glad when it's over."

"Me too," Neil said. He put his arm around her

waist. It felt good. Clare cuddled up to him. They sat like that for a while, not speaking. An old Al Green tape was on the stereo, one that Neil had made for her when they were going out, *Greatest Hits Volumes 1 & 2*. He'd tried to use it as a seduction aid on more than one occasion, nearly succeeded.

"I suppose I ought to call a taxi," Neil said, when the last song finished. "I'll come for the car in the morning, give you a lift to work."

"Don't go just yet," Clare said. "Turn the tape over."

"OK," Neil said, giving her an odd look.

Clare knew that she was giving out mixed signals, but didn't care. She was drunk and emotional and she was tired of being alone. She needed to be held.

"Let's dance," she said. "I like this one a lot."

"Me too," Neil muttered, as he gripped her tightly and she buried her head in his chest, realizing how much she'd missed the feel of a man, the promise of sex.

Later, when she woke at six with her head pounding and Neil naked beside her, Clare knew that she'd made a mistake. But while it was happening, while they were dancing and kissing and cuddling and making tender, drunken love, it had been lovely. Clare tried to remember that as she stumbled down to the kitchen, took two solpadeines and drank a pint of water with lots of ice. She worried for a moment that she had betrayed Paul, not long in his grave. But she and Neil had not really made love, they had had sex. There was nothing to feel guilty about. Even so, she wondered what on earth she would say to Neil when he woke.

Chris got up at eleven. He had a hangover, as he usually did on Sundays. This one was made worse by his not having slept much, despite the comfortable king-size bed. Lynda was in the shower. When the doorbell rang, Chris assumed that it was room service with their breakfast. Instead, it was Jane Waverly, the production's stage manager. She didn't appear to recognize Dylan, but didn't seem surprised to find him there, either.

"Is Lynda here?"

"In the shower."

"Could you get her, please?"

"Wouldn't it be easier if I gave her a message?"

"No," Jane said. "I think I'd better tell her this personally."

Lynda grinned as he pulled back the shower curtain. "You're insatiable, you are."

"Not this time," Chris said. "It's someone about work." She put on a towelling dressing-gown then walked, dripping, into the bedroom.

"Change of plan?" she asked Jane.

"I'm afraid so," the stage manager told her. "The rest of the run's been cancelled. All the bad publicity has meant lousy ticket sales and…"

"You're kidding!" Lynda said. "This is my big break. You can't take it away!"

"Not my decision, sorry."

"Then whose? I want to see them *now*!"

"Hey, calm down," Jane said. "I understand you're upset, Lynda, but think about it. You can't expect an audience to pay top prices to see two understudies in starring roles. Anyway, the play carrying on would be ghoulish. Paul and Trudy agreed to cancel after last night's performance. You'll still get paid for the remaining two weeks of the tour."

"At the understudy rate!"

"Well, yes," Jane said, frowning and looking at her watch. "Look, I have to find the others. You've got to vacate your suite by twelve, Lynda. Again, I'm sorry. I hope we get to work together again." She exited quickly. Chris tried to comfort Lynda, but she was too angry to listen to him. When room service wheeled in the breakfast, she lost it altogether.

"How could they do this?" she yelled. "It's not fair! All those years of crap parts, waiting for a break…"

"You'll get another break," Chris tried to tell her.

"Like hell I will. I've seen it happen again and again. Women get to my age and they haven't made it. Suddenly the parts are thinner on the ground. Next thing you know, they get married, then go into teaching or have babies. By the time they're forty they're saying *I used to be an actress*. I'm not having that!"

"Let's have some breakfast," Chris suggested.

"I don't want breakfast!" she shouted, and began to throw the food around the room. Bacon and eggs spattered the bed. The coffee pot lost its contents all over the carpet. Croissants crumbled against the bedroom mirror. Chris felt a terrible sense of *déjà vu*. His ex-wife used to have tantrums like this.

After a while, Lynda calmed down enough for him to persuade her to pack.

"We ought to get out of here before they send a chambermaid to clean up. I'm sure the theatre'll pay for the mess."

"They'd better, after what they've done to me!"

"I'll ring the station, find out what time the next London train is."

"Doesn't matter," Lynda mumbled, as though sensing the futility of venting her anger on Chris. "I've got my car. You go. I can sort myself out."

"Don't be daft," Chris told her, tenderly. "Let me help you pack." Reluctantly, she allowed him to find the bits and pieces she had scattered around the room. Lynda was the messiest person that Chris had ever come across. He was beginning to reconsider continuing his affair with her.

"You go to work," she said, when her bags were ready.

"It's all right," he told her. "You'll hurt yourself, carrying that lot."

"I'll get a porter."

"Then he'll see what a mess you've made of the room. C'mon, leave the key in the door. Let's just go." Reluctantly, she agreed. They took the lift down to the underground car park. It was a grey mausoleum, eerily lit like a road tunnel.

"Which is yours?" Chris asked, and Lynda pointed at an ageing Peugeot 309, its front facing the far corner of the car park, its sills muddy. The car didn't appear to have been washed for a long time.

"Could you open the boot?" Chris asked. He was carrying the two heaviest bags.

"They can go on the back seat," Lynda told him.

"The boot'd be a lot easier." There was another car parked tightly next to hers, making access awkward.

"Oh, all right." Lynda unlocked the boot, which was empty, apart from some crumpled newspapers. As Chris put Lynda's bags in, he realized that the back seat was loose. It was one of those seats that you could fold down to create extra space in the back. Chris knew this model, used to own one which his ex-wife had ended up with. He could see that the rear seats hadn't been put back properly. One of the rear seat-belts had got in the way. All Chris had to do to fix it was to pull a lever, tug the seat-belt away from the socket, then push the seat back into place.

As Chris moved the seat-belt, his hand brushed against something in the seat lock cavity. He went to wipe it, then saw what the *something* was. A few strands of hair. Human hair, he was pretty sure. The light was bad, but it looked like dark hair. Not brown, like Lynda's, but nearly black, like…

"Would you mind dropping me off at the station?" he asked, casually.

"Whatever," Lynda said, throwing in the final bag and slamming shut the boot. Cautiously, Chris got into the passenger seat.

23

Neil and Clare reported for work at midday, as the DI had requested. They didn't talk on the way in. Neil had woken in the night. At first he'd thought that he was with Melanie. She was holding on to him and felt heavier than usual. Then he'd tried to get out of bed and found a wall where there shouldn't be one. Only then did his eyes become accustomed to the darkness.

Coming back from the toilet, he thought about dressing, getting in his car, going home. For months and months, he had tried to persuade Clare to sleep with him, but she would never go all the way, saying that she had to be sure she was in *love*. Yet, last night, she had come on to him. He, after a mere token hesitation, had succumbed. They had used each other's bodies casually, for comfort. Clare was not in love with him, never would be. And Neil, he realized, was not in love with Clare any more. He was still in love with Melanie. He wanted to get her back.

Neil drank some water. He couldn't drive. He was still drunk. So he had got back in bed next to Clare and, somehow, eventually, he slept again. Now it was five to twelve and his head was throbbing. Since getting up, neither he nor Clare had discussed the night before. Maybe they never would.

As Neil pulled up, Lynda Crabbe was dropping off Chris Dylan outside the station. Neil wasn't the only one who'd got lucky last night. Instead of going inside, Chris pointed at the back of Lynda's car. He seemed to be telling Lynda that something was wrong with her car. Seeing Neil, he beckoned him over, an urgent look on his face.

"What's going on?" Clare asked, her first words since she'd got in the car.

"Dunno. I'd better go." Neil ran over to Chris. Lynda was still parked, looking confused.

"What is it?" Neil asked Chris.

"I'm pretending to see a bad oil leak, which I'm going to get sorted out. I want you to tell Lynda that you have a few questions before she leaves town, save her time later. No big deal. All right?"

"All right, anything you say," Neil told him, confused. After Chris had spun his story about the oil leak, Lynda got out of the car. She was about to look at the problem when Neil intercepted her.

"Lynda, I'm really glad you're here. Look, I know it's a nuisance but the boss wants me to go over your statement yet again. We're doing it with all the main witnesses. It'll take half an hour, save you coming back later."

"Looks like I have to hang around anyhow," Lynda said, looking at her car before letting Neil lead her to an interview room, where he left her.

"What the hell's going on?" Neil asked, joining the others in the incident room.

"We're sending for Forensics," Greasby told him. "Chris thinks he's found our killer."

Chris, forced to admit that he'd been sleeping with a key suspect, was not allowed in on Lynda Crabbe's interview, even though he was the one who'd found the crucial lead. Neil went instead, backing up John Greasby.

Chris *was* allowed to listen to the tape afterwards. The confession came after twenty minutes, when Lynda got tired of stonewalling.

Neil was the one who finally got to her.

"We found some hair in the back of your car, Lynda. It doesn't look like yours. Forensics are examining it now. Within the hour, they'll be able to tell us whether it belongs to Anna Derbyshire or not. And if it's Anna's hair, there'll be other traces of her body, too."

"Anna's been in my car."

"In the boot?" Neil again. Lynda didn't respond.

"They'll also be examining mud residues on your sills and tyres," Greasby went on, "checking them against the building site where the body was found. You're not going to get away with it. Why don't you save some time by telling us what happened?" Lynda was quiet. The silence lasted nearly a minute before Neil broke it.

"How did you find that building site?"

"Dumb luck," Lynda said, after a pause.

"Pardon?" Neil. And suddenly it all came out.

"I was driving around with the body, meaning to drop it in the river. It was nearly six. I only had an hour before I had to be in the theatre, but I didn't want to leave Anna in the car for a second night. I was heading to Trent Bridge when I noticed the building site. It looked deserted, so I decided to steal bricks or something to weight the body down."

"Then you changed your mind?" Neil.

"While I was looking for the bricks I came across this big pool of concrete, newly poured, not far from the car. So I dragged Anna out of the back of the car, stuffed bits of brick into her leather jacket and threw her in."

"On your own?" Greasby.

"Yes. I'm strong for my size. But the body didn't

sink, hardly at all. I tried poking it with a stick and it went down a little. It was dark. I figured it would go all the way under by morning, so I left." In fact, it had taken until ten before the body was completely submerged.

"You're admitting to the murder of Anna Derbyshire?" Greasby.

"Not much point in denying it, is there? You've got enough evidence."

"Where did you do it?" Neil.

"In the car."

"Take us back," Greasby said. "Give us the full story."

Lynda drew breath, then started. "On Thursday, I persuaded Anna to go for a drive to Wollaton Park, take a look around. When we were there, I put a couple of my sleeping pills into her drink. She was soon feeling ill, thought she was coming down with something. So, before I drove her back, I suggested she write a note to Paul, warning him that she might not be well enough to make that night's performance. She fell asleep before she finished it. I had to forge the ending, making it look like she was quitting the production. Then I drove around until I found a deserted car park, dragged her into the back of the car and strangled her. The rest you know."

"All this just to get her part?" Greasby asked, incredulous.

"Why not?" Lynda said, calmly. "I saw what happened to Jeremy. Only twenty and getting good TV offers, all because of Mark Murray being murdered. Why shouldn't it happen for me, too?"

"But Jeremy didn't commit murder to get the part." Neil.

"How do you know? Do you know who killed Mark?"

"Did you do it?" Greasby.

"I might have done, for all you know. There's no evidence against anyone, is there? If I hadn't been hungover and angry, I'd never have let Chris near my car, and you wouldn't have any evidence against me, either. You didn't even know that I had a car, did you?"

"No," Greasby admitted.

"Well, then."

"Lynda Crabbe, I am charging you with the murder of Anna Derbyshire. You do not have to say anything, but if you do not mention now something which you later use in your defence…"

Chris turned off the tape. Two killings. One result. Half a job done. That was something. He wondered whether Lynda had slept with him in order to deflect attention from herself as a suspect, or because she really wanted to. That first time they were together, she had made a joke about him being her alibi, when all the time, Anna's body had been in her car.

It was creepy, having been with a murderer. Maybe his ex-wife had been right. Casual sex was never really casual. Chris doubted that they would ever discover who had killed Mark Murray, but he would bet his every penny that it was a vengeful woman. The world was full of ones to choose from.

EPILOGUE

Clare was already late for her drink with Charlene when a woman arrived at the station, demanding to speak with someone from CID. Everyone else had knocked off early, so Clare went down to see her. The woman was twenty something, tall and beautiful, but brittle looking. There was something familiar about her.

"Gill Smart," she said, introducing herself.

"Do I know you?" Clare asked.

"My maiden name was Crane."

Clare tried to stay composed. "Oh yes," she said. "We've been looking for you."

"I've been away – a week in Gran Canaria. Got back today. A friend told me that you were asking about me. She also told me about my sister." Gill

Crane was Tamara's sister. She was supposed to have killed herself. She was also supposed to be the woman Mark had met in the restaurant, the one they'd been looking for for a week. Maybe she had come to confess to killing Mark.

"I read in this evening's paper that you let my sister go."

"Yes," Clare said, carefully. "She was released yesterday."

"Why?"

Clare hesitated. "I'm not sure I can reveal…"

Gill's face flushed angrily. "She's my sister. She confessed to killing my ex-boyfriend. So I think you ought to tell me, why did you let Tamara go?"

"She withdrew her confession," Clare revealed. "We have no other evidence."

"Do you know why I finished with Mark?" Gill asked, scowling.

"No." Clare thought that it was the other way round, but kept quiet.

"I found him in bed with Tamara. She'd just turned fifteen at the time. He always had a thing about young girls, but it never occurred to me that she'd betray me that way. I'd gone out shopping, got back early. You know what the worst thing was? My mum took Tamara's side. It was my fault for bringing Mark into the house. How could she resist him, the poor thing? We had a big falling out."

"I see," Clare said. "What happened next?"

"I haven't seen my mum or Tamara from that day to this."

"That seems a little … extreme," Clare said. Was any man worth losing your family over?

"Does it? I wanted to spend the rest of my life with Mark. Instead, I stayed in Nottingham, got married on the rebound. My husband adores me, but it's not a very good marriage."

"Tell me what happened last week," Clare said, still not sure whether a confession might be coming.

"When I heard that Mark was in Nottingham, I wrote, arranged to meet him. I wanted to know if he knew how much he'd hurt us, how he'd destroyed our family. Of course, he hadn't the least idea. Oh, he apologized for screwing Tamara. Mark said it meant nothing. She'd thrown herself at him. He could hardly remember her. You know what the worst thing was?"

"Tell me."

"The other night, when we met, he turned up at the restaurant with a young girl, fifteen at most. And before he came in, he kissed her, for a long time, in full view of where I was sitting. Can you guess how humiliating that was?"

"Is that why you killed him?" Clare boldly asked.

"Killed him?" Gill sneered condescendingly. "You're barking up the wrong tree. Tamara killed Mark."

"Why?" The revenge motive made no sense now that Gill was still alive.

"Because of what he did to our family."

"That doesn't seem a big enough motive for murder," Clare said.

"You don't know my family." Gill's voice rose. "I can imagine the way the hatred built up. Tamara probably convinced herself that everything that happened was all Mark's fault. And then to watch him, getting more and more successful – that tore me up, I'll tell you. It must have done the same to Tamara, and Mum. I'll tell you something else, too. I hate her and Mum more than I hated Mark. Mark was what he was. But they're my family and they betrayed me, both of them."

"I see," Clare said, unsettled by the venom in Gill's voice. If hatred like this ran in the family, then, yes, maybe there was enough motive for Tamara to have killed Mark. "If you're right," she said to Gill, "why did Tamara confess?"

"Maybe she thought it'd make me come forward, forgive her and my mum. They spent ages looking for me, but my friends wouldn't tell them where I was."

"They said they thought that you'd committed suicide."

Gill shook her head. "They know that isn't true. Tamara kept coming to Nottingham, looking for me. I heard from a friend that she was here again.

That was why I took the last minute holiday in Gran Canaria."

"I'd like to see the tickets, if you have them." Gill produced her boarding passes from a handbag. The dates were right. Gill had been out of the country by the time that Mark was murdered.

"Did you warn Mark about Tamara being in town?" Clare asked.

"No. Why should I?"

Clare pressed. "Wouldn't you have done, if you'd known what Tamara was going to do?"

Gill Crane gave her a cold look. "What kind of a question is that? What I want to know is: are you going to charge her?"

"We've already done that once, then dropped the charges," Clare explained. "To do it again, we need proof. Real proof. You've given us a motive, but, without evidence, it isn't enough."

"She did it. I'll bet Mum knows, too." Clare would bet that she did, too. Now that the dust was settling on this case, that was the only explanation which made sense. But how would they prove it? Samantha Crane had provided her youngest daughter with a partial alibi. No one remembered selling Tamara the murder weapon. There was no evidence.

The case wasn't over. The police could still charge Tamara, use her own words against her. They could try and find new witnesses. But Tamara would be well trained now. She would not confess again. Unless there was something they'd missed, there really wasn't enough evidence to justify a second charge. And the police would never know if Tamara Crane had killed Mark Murray, not for sure.

"I need to hand you over to a senior officer," Clare said. She got hold of John Greasby at home, just as he walked through his front door. He didn't seem too surprised by what Clare had to tell him. Clare put on her coat and headed for the Playhouse bar, her head reeling.

Ian Jagger must have worked it out early on, Clare reckoned. Jagger would have persuaded Tamara to fudge some of the details in her second interview. The solicitor had made his client delay, then urged her to withdraw her confession at the crucial moment, when the police's attention was on Anna Derbyshire's death. Tamara, having got all the anger out of her system, had played along. She'd got what she wanted, destroying Mark's reputation. There was no need for her to go to prison, not when a clever lawyer could get her off.

Was Mark as bad as Gill made out? DNA tests had confirmed that Anna Derbyshire was carrying Mark Murray's baby – he hadn't done so badly there. So he had made passes at a few women who weren't interested. So what? Mark had never harassed anyone or promised them parts if they slept with him. Tamara Crane had been under age, true, but it didn't sound like the fault was all on Mark's side. Tamara was a jealous, headstrong girl who wanted to steal her sister's lover. Moreover, Mark hadn't tried to seduce the fourteen-year-old Jo McCord, although it sounded like he'd been tempted to. Maybe his restraint demonstrated that he'd grown up, or, at least, learnt a little.

In the end, all that Mark could be found guilty of was exploiting his good looks and cheating on a girlfriend or two. This was something that most men would do, if they thought they wouldn't have to pay a price. Clare had been too hard on Mark, she decided, partly because he was successful, and – all right, yes – partly because he had never made a second pass at her when she was a teenager, a pass which she might have treated differently from the first one.

Clare had been wrong about Tamara, too. She'd seen that the girl was unbalanced, but thought her a fake. Some detective she was! Clare wondered if Charlene had been in on the clever manoeuvring which Jagger had accomplished. Not that Charlene would tell her. This was a big achievement, even for Jagger, getting the police to drop the charges against a confessed murderer. If Gill was right, Tamara Crane had killed one person, and indirectly caused the death of another. And, just like the person who had killed Clare's lover, she was going to get away with it.

The roads were quiet. Most people had finished work, but it was too early for others to be heading back into town, for the clubs, pubs and cinemas. The pavements were quiet too. The city felt safe. It felt like home. Then the rain began, and Clare walked faster, her ankle aching a little as she stepped up the pace.

There was no justice to be had, Clare realized, taking the subway beneath Maid Marion Way to avoid the drizzle. There would be no satisfying solution. Clare had to go back on the beat tomorrow, and she was dreading it. Maybe she was in the wrong job.

Have you read the other titles in THE BEAT series...?

Avenging Angel

Introducing Clare Coppola, Neil Foster and Jan Hunt...

When Angelo Coppola is tragically killed in a hit-and-run accident, the police are unable to track down the culprit.

But Angelo's sister, Clare, cannot rest till she has discovered the truth. Who was driving the car that killed him? And what is the significance of "blaze" – the last word that Angelo uttered?

Clare is soon convinced that she has found the killer. But can she prove it? And is she putting her own life in danger?

Missing Person

Introducing Ben Shipman, Ruth Clarke, Sam Holt and Steve Garrett...

Fifteen-year-old Hannah Brown is missing – just another teenage runaway. Or is she?

Only PC Clare Coppola, working on her first police case, thinks otherwise. But how can she prove that Hannah is in danger? And what connection can a missing teenager have with a spate of local burglaries?

Black and Blue

Introducing Ted Sutcliffe and Ian Jagger...

Violence is brewing on Ben's beat – deliberate, organized violence. But who is behind it, and what are they trying to achieve?

Ben is determined to find out. And he's got more than just a professional interest – because some of the violence is directed against *him*. Being a black police officer could be harder than he thought...

Smokescreen

Introducing Chris Dylan and Charlene Harris...

There's a serial arsonist at large, going by the name of *Phoenix*. First Clare's school is burnt down, then the local library. What will be the next target?

Now Neil has been transferred to CID, Clare is determined to prove her worth and find Phoenix. But how can she track down an arsonist who's as elusive as a puff of smoke?

Asking For It

Introducing Paul Grace and Melanie Byatt...

A thirteen-year-old girl has been raped, and Neil is assigned to the case. Then there's a second rape. This time a student. And the man wore a mask.

Could the two crimes be linked? Or is it just coincidence?

Neil is determined to find out. But if the rapist isn't caught soon, he could attack again...

Dead White Male

Introducing Gary Monk...

When nineteen-year-old Scott Travis is found battered to death, the police are baffled. What motive could there be for such chilling violence?

But as Clare delves deeper into the victim's past, small clues begin to come to light. Clues linking a student, an ex-prostitute and a police officer in a web of lies and deceit. Could one of them have killed to keep their secret hidden...?

Losers

The first of three novels featuring the gang known as the Motorway Team, and introducing the Wilder family and Eddie Brown...

Life on the Maynard Estate is hard, and Julie Wilder wants out. A winning scratchcard could be her ticket to a new life...

A life such as Gordon Loscoe's. He won the Lottery and lives in the lap of luxury. That is, until his house is burgled and his wife is violently abducted...

Called in to investigate, Paul and Clare uncover a network of crime based on greed and betrayal. But proving it could be quite a gamble...

Sudden Death

When Dean Sutherland gets picked to play for Nottingham Forest, he's over the moon. It means a whole new start. Of course, he's always been into team games, just not always *legitimate* ones...

Deans old friends are not so happy, though. They think he owes them something, and there's only one way he can pay. But now he's sharing a house with a police officer, he has to be careful. Neil Foster's no fool...

As the motorway team move in for another big-time burglary, Dean has to decide which side he's on. Whichever he chooses, there'll be a penalty to pay.

Night Shift

The motorway team are still at large, but a key witness is behind bars. The police are just waiting for him to sing like a bird…

But Joe isn't stupid. He knows what happens to people who cross the team. they end up dead. As least no one can touch him while he's inside.

Back at the station, the night shift is beginning. That means eight long hours on duty for Clare – her first shift after the funeral. Eight hours during which anything can happen. Like a prison break in…

Victims

Events from Ruth's past come back to haunt her final appearance in the series…

Alan Wallace has just got off scot-free. The locals are outraged. But the police are duty bound to protect everyone. Even perverts…

Then a two-year-old boy goes missing. According to the police, Wallace is not a suspect. But the community's not so sure…

When justice fails, do you turn the other cheek? Or take the law into your own hands? Because shouldn't the punishment always fit the crime…?

and coming soon…

Fallen Angel

Jo McCord thinks she's found love, but there's a dark side to her new boyfriend she never could have imagined…

Ben Shipman is determined to pin something on Ian Jagger before the slippery lawyer ties the knot with Charlene…

And Clare's probationary period comes to an end. Suddenly, her biggest decision is not whether to stay in the police force…